Operation Samarium

CARLOS USÍN

ISBN-13: 9788835447955

RPI: M-002157/2022

Cover design: Marta Fernández García

Translator: Amanda Witan

Carlos Usín

DEDICATION

For Cuchy

Contents

Operation Samarium

THANKS

I want to express my sincere gratitude to my friend and fellow writer Mercedes Freedman.

She has contributed selflessly and with her usual enthusiasm to refine this novel, using her knowledge, her acute sense of critique and her immense ability to delve deep into the text and develop its full potential.

I have always admired her, not only for her finesse in writing, but also for her incredible flair for discovering the most unsuspected nuances however elusive they may seem.

Operation Samarium

1. The theft

Under the cover of darkness, the two men had no trouble leaving the house, unobserved by anyone. It was early morning and the quiet calm of the neighbourhood was only disturbed by a few crickets. They walked slowly towards their security van, parked in front of the main entrance of the villa, one of the many in this luxury private estate designed exclusively for the rich and powerful of Marbella.

All the security cameras in the house had been disabled, just as they had been told they would be. The only evidence the police would later glean from them was two uniformed security guards carrying out a routine inspection of one of the properties.

No one would have suspected, even if there had been direct witnesses, that under his uniform one of them was hiding a work of art worth more than sixty million euros, owned by a wealthy businessman named Aaron Bukowski. They, of course, had been kept in the dark as to the identity of the owner and indeed the true value of what they had stolen.

As they drove back to the checkpoint to end their shift, they both agreed that they found it astonishing that so many security measures had achieved nothing. Nor did they understand why such a small drawing – a mere 40 x 30 centimetres – had been targeted, when they saw much larger pictures on the walls that were surely worth far more.

Up to that point, everything had gone smoothly and in exact accordance with the plan they had been instructed to follow. Thanks to the maps they had been given, they easily identified the private estate, its location and the villa to be burgled. They turned up dead on time. They presented their fake ID cards at the checkpoint, signed in and set out to do the job of patrolling, which would conceal their real intentions. At the appointed time, they went to the designated property. They entered with the key they had been given and found the picture in the place that had been indicated. They took it, wrapped it up as they had been told to do, left the house, got into the security van, finished their shift and signed out. They drove to the place they had been ordered to make the exchange in the same van they had used to get to the residential estate. This vehicle had been provided to them the day before with precise instructions to use it exclusively for this job.

As they drove to the site chosen for the handover, Vasili, who was driving, began to have second thoughts. He was growing nervous and all types of dreadful scenarios were passing through his mind. He should have thought about it before accepting the job, but the smell of the money they had been promised was too much of a temptation for any objective consideration.

The truth was, they knew damn all about this individual they were about to meet, and that was a risk. They were told that it was an insurance scam, that in exchange for the stolen picture they would be given two envelopes, each containing two thousand five hundred euros, the remaining half of the agreed money.

While he was brooding on this, he turned to his friend, sat in the passenger seat:

'What if this guy puts a couple of bullets into us to take us out of the picture?' he blurted out.

'It's a bit late to think about that now, isn't it?' Grigori replied, looking alarmed. 'What can we do? We've got no weapons and neither of us has ever killed anyone.'

'You're right, there's nothing we can do, except pray. Are you any good at praying, Grigori?'

Grigori stared at him, saying nothing, feeling a mixture of concern and sympathy. He never imagined that his companion would end up thinking about praying to save his own skin. Vasili was always the one who took the initiative, who invariably saw the bright side of things, who came up with the most ingenious solutions to problems. He was his friend, yes, but he was also his mentor. And now he was talking about praying. He must have been really scared and that just wasn't like him.

Vasili continued blathering on, which made it clear to Grigori that his pal was indeed genuinely afraid. He only did that when he was really worried and things were getting out of hand.

'Well, at least we know that the guy who hired us is called Oleg.'

'Take it easy, Vasili. Sometimes I think you're losing it. Let's just look at things calmly. Firstly, that's not going to be much use to you if you're dead.'

'You're right about that.'

'And if we live to tell the tale, I think you'd better forget about him. He's not the kind of guy I'd like to have on my back.'

'Yeah, you're right about that too.'

'Secondly, are you sure his name is Oleg? A guy who broke into our house, who knows where we live, who knows our phone numbers and who got us perfectly fitting uniforms, just to steal a small picture, worth who knows how much, is he going to tell you his real name?'

'You're right, Grigori.'

After a brief pause, Grigori thought that Vasili had got a grip on himself and accepting that the die had been cast, had calmed down and would shut up. But he was wrong.

'And Marina? Her name was Marina, wasn't it? You know, that

waitress from the club. God, I've never seen longer legs in my life! Did you see her tits? She was hot, huh?'

Once again, Grigori gave him a concerned look. His friend was trying to escape from reality, dreaming of a woman who was only available to millionaires and classy people. In addition, Oleg had already made it clear to them that this waitress was his property. You could tell by the way he gave her instructions, with a simple nod, and because at the end of their meeting he had warned them both that she was out of bounds.

'Vasili, listen to me, that guy Oleg or whatever his name is, told you to forget about her. And you'd better do it. That little beauty wouldn't even say good morning to you. She's out of your league.'

Finally, they arrived at the spot where the exchange was to take place. It was a relatively remote area and at that time of day there was nothing going on. What's more, they didn't know the individual by sight, they had just been told to wait for someone.

Suddenly, there was a flash of headlights from among the parked cars and they headed that way. Vasili stopped the car, about ten metres from the other vehicle. It was a distance he considered prudent and safe in case of complications. Then a man got out of the other car and walked straight towards them with his hands in his jacket pockets.

'Vasili.'

'What?'

'Tell me it's going to be alright.'

'I hope so, Grigori. I bloody hope so. But just in case, I want you to know that you are the best mate ever.'

'And you feel you have to tell me that at this precise moment?'

The man approached the car. Bending down, he looked at the men inside, still dressed in their security guard uniforms. Vasili and Grigori were scared to death. And the fake smile of the man standing at their window did nothing to reassure them.

'*Privet*,' he greeted them in Russian.

'*Privet*,' Vasili responded.

Then Vasili turned around, took the stolen goods from the back seat and handed it over to the stranger. The man took his hands out of his pockets and without even verifying the package, reached into the inside pocket of his jacket. At that moment, Grigori and Vasili both flinched and for a few seconds wondered whether to knock the guy out and run away, saying goodbye to the money, or whether they should beg for mercy. They were sure he was about to pull out a gun with a silencer and they would be found rigid and dead the next morning. Vasili's idea of praying didn't seem so stupid now, though it sure as hell wasn't going to save their skins. In any case, Grigori was as good as praying, repeating over and over to himself something his mother had taught him as a child.

The guy did not pull out a weapon. Instead, he handed them two envelopes. They looked in them and found two thousand five hundred euros in each. He got into his car and drove off. They both took a deep breath. Their legs were shaking and their hearts were beating so fast they felt like they would burst. They would have given anything to have a shot of vodka at that moment. But the job wasn't over yet.

When they had caught their breath a little, following the instructions they had been given, they changed out of their uniforms leaving them in the car that had been provided and putting on their own clothes which they had left in Vasili's car, parked there the day before.

'Grigori.'

'Yes?'

'We need new phone numbers.'

'Yeah, I know.'

'Burners, I reckon.'

'Sure.'

'And we need to move house.'

'Yeah, I agree. I'm not having Oleg, or whatever his name is, rummaging through my wardrobe again.'

They took the SIMs out of their mobiles and threw them out of the window.

'OK, then. Where do we go from here?'

'No idea. Any suggestions?'

'No. But anywhere's better than here.'

Vasili started the engine and they headed for the motorway, with no clear plan, but in the direction of Algeciras. All they wanted to do was get the hell out of there as soon as possible. Then Vasili saw the headlights of a car in the rear-view mirror. He hadn't seen anyone arrive while they were stopped. In other words, whoever it was, had already been there keeping watch. Vasili kept his eyes on the mirror, but without saying anything to his friend, who hadn't noticed anything. Finally, just before they merged onto the motorway, the ghost car turned and Vasili took a deep breath. They were not being followed. Or so it appeared.

***

The man now in possession of the stolen picture went directly to Puerto Banús following the orders he had been given. When he arrived, he left the car he had been given and walked to the pontoon they had specified. A huge yacht was moored there, with the name *IRINA* in gold letters on the side. That was the spot where the handover was to take place.

He approached the access ladder at the stern of the boat. As he set foot on the first step, several figures appeared on the deck at the top of the ladder. The one who appeared to be the boss was protected by three others standing behind him, all of them giant short-necked monsters with enough weapons to launch an invasion. The man figured that every one of those necks was pretty much the width of his thighs. They must have weighed a hundred and thirty kilos each and stood about two metres tall. Their suits looked as if they were about to burst open at any moment. The whole effect was unsettling, and if that wasn't intimidating enough, he wasn't reassured by the distrustful looks that greeted him. But he couldn't back out now. He climbed to the top of the ladder. All he had to do was complete the job: deliver a package. That's what he did. No one said a word. In return, the boss handed him an envelope, then turned away while his bodyguards stood there waiting for the visitor to leave. He, too, turned away from the gorillas with a slight nod of his head, accompanied by a forced smile, half out of politeness, half out of panic. It was only when he stepped back onto dry land that the heavies withdrew inside the yacht. He opened the envelope and checked that the money was as agreed and headed for a taxi. His job was done.

The head man made a phone call to report back and get further instructions.

'You already know what you have to do,' was the order he received.

'Very good, sir.'

He hung up and went to find the captain in his cabin. He knocked, and the captain, looking sleepy, opened the door.

'We're leaving, Captain.'

'Destination?'

'Monte Carlo.'

'Very well, sir. We'll be departing in a short while.'

After shaking himself awake and putting on his uniform, the captain made his way to the bridge, rousing the rest of the crew as he went. While he waited for them to arrive, he poured himself a strong cup of coffee and spent a few minutes checking instruments and charts and calculating how long the trip would take.

The yacht *Irina* was one of those vessels that attracted attention wherever it docked. Its three decks and forty metres length provided comfortable accommodation for ten passengers and eight crew members, not to mention the owner's extravagances, including a sauna and gold bathroom fittings.

The captain checked the radio and confirmed that all the instrumentation was functioning correctly. Then he calculated the time of arrival. Her two diesel engines with a total capacity of six thousand horsepower gave her a top speed of twenty-five knots, without pushing it to the limit. Her diesel tanks, filled to the brim, held up to twenty-nine thousand litres, giving her full range to make the journey without stopovers.

Ahead of them lay some seven hundred miles of sailing through a calm autumn Mediterranean, which meant almost two days of voyage at an average speed of seventeen knots.

The night was warm, the sky was full of stars and the weather forecast indicated that the sea would be calm. It would be a peaceful crossing, although it was important to keep an eye out for the surprises that night at sea can bring: boats full of immigrants trying to reach the Spanish coast, others lost and without bearings, smugglers speeding across with their powerful outboards in search of the mother ship, all of them without running lights.

But none of that could hinder or slow the yacht's progress. The instructions were clear and precise.

2. Grigori and Vasili

Once they had exchanged the merchandise for money and checked that no one was following them, Vasili seemed calmer. In fact, the irrepressible jabbering of earlier was replaced by complete silence, much to Grigori's relief. It meant he could snatch a quick nap.

While Vasili was driving the car to get them away from Marbella, he considered how they had got themselves into this dodgy situation and embarked on a review of recent events. At this time of day, traffic was non-existent and he was cruising at a moderate speed, so he could let his mind wander.

The range of possibilities for entertainment offered to Grigori and Vasili was fairly limited. It basically depended on their financial resources, which fluctuated between meagre and pitiful. Their usual habit - if the budget did not allow for more, which was most of the time - was to go into a bar and drink a few beers while watching a football match on TV. If their finances were a bit more buoyant, they could replace beer with vodka, albeit cheap and of abysmal quality. Only occasionally, and under certain special, infrequent and singular circumstances, could they afford to treat themselves to a visit to a nightclub, striptease included, even if the dancers were a little well upholstered and had probably left their grandchildren in the care of a neighbour.

So it was that on that Thursday, one rash midweek day, they decided to go to San Pedro de Alcantara and treat themselves to a special night out. Little did they imagine what they were about to get involved in.

While they were enjoying the spectacle - sad, decadent and pathetic - drinking a third-rate vodka and hoping to be able to convince one of the women in the room to have sex at a reasonable price, a guy came up to their table.

The man, whom they had never seen there before, started talking to them, commenting on the strippers' bodies and in particular their tits. Then, out of the blue, he made them a proposition:

> 'Would you like to earn yourselves some easy cash? Then you could up your game and fuck a far classier tart than any of these here.'

The idea of being able to afford a whore that was above their usual standard got them on the hook. Besides, the stranger had told them that it would be easy money. They wanted to believe him.

The man had style. He spoke with an educated accent that sounded like it was from eastern Europe, although they couldn't be sure he was Russian. He was no small-time punk. He dressed well, in an expensive suit, so he must be successful in business and know how to earn a penny. In fact, they wondered how such an individual, looking like that, had stumbled into a dump like that.

The stranger invited them to discuss the matter further, but in a more discreet place.

> 'Do you have a car?'

> 'Yes.'

> 'Good. Follow me, please.'

They left the nightclub and watched as their new friend got into his car, an 800hp V-12 Lamborghini Aventador. They followed him in theirs, a second-hand Audi A4. He drove to Puerto Banús.

The club he took them to was right in front of the marina. Stopping at the entrance, they left the cars with the valet and went inside. A huge bouncer, his head shaved like a billiard ball, stood at the door, checking out the visitors. When he saw who it was, he let them through and greeted their new friend as if he knew him and he was there frequently.

'Come with me,' the man ordered, as the gorilla gave a nod indicating that he understood the situation.

The place was called *Irina la dulce*, which was either a demonstration of the owner's lack of imagination when looking for a name, or else a subtle irony with reference to the film *Irma la Douce* (Irma, the sweet one) in which the main character was a prostitute. In any case, Grigori and Vasili had never even heard of Jack Lemmon or Shirley MacLaine and had certainly never seen the film.

After passing the payment booth, they had to climb a staircase with a dozen or so steps, at the top of which there were security staff controlling access. Behind them were huge, heavy velvet curtains whose main function was to isolate the noise, ensure the privacy of the guests and maintain an intimate atmosphere. Behind these curtains and down three steps, you reached the restaurant area with a small number of tables and a bar on the left where you could have a drink.

The club was tall and spacious, in the shape of a huge barrel. At the far end was a brightly lit stage, with a central pole, where a topless dancer gyrated and performed intricate erotic moves to the rhythm of the music. In between the restaurant and the stage, there were tables arranged in a semi-circle where you could take your time to relax and enjoy a drink while watching the show.

As soon as they walked in, they could see that there was a big difference between the strippers they were used to and the 'escorts' that filled every corner of this club. Booths were located on the sides of the long barrel, to the left and right. They had curtains drawn across for privacy and a guard outside to ensure that nobody interrupted what was taking place inside.

The type of clientele was also very different. They looked like powerful businessmen, with a lot of money and an even greater desire to show that they had it. You only had to check out the cars parked around the place. They were a lot fancier than the ones they were used to seeing in the dives they frequented.

Their host was perfectly at ease in this establishment. It was obvious that he knew it well or might even be the owner or at least the manager. There were plenty of clues; the way the bouncer at the door greeted him, the reaction of the waiters and the girls when they saw him arrive and the manner in which he moved around without the slightest hesitation. What they did not understand was why a man with a car like that and associated with a place like this, would go out of his way to seek them out. Before the end of the night, they would understand his motives.

He took them to an office tucked away from inquisitive eyes, situated at the far end, to the right of the stage. Inside, it was so well soundproofed that they could barely hear the music accompanying the exotic dancer on stage. They could observe her perfectly through a viewing window, which allowed them to see the show from there without being observed from the other side. They sat on a crescent-shaped leather sofa facing the entertainment. No sooner had they made themselves comfortable than a waitress appeared who left the two guests with their mouths hanging open. She must have been six feet tall with blonde, shoulder-length hair, almond green eyes and amazingly long legs. She wore a miniskirt that covered very little and a white blouse, under which there was nothing but her bare breasts. Her chest must have been at least a size thirty-eight.

'What would you like to drink, gentlemen?'

They would have liked to answer with the sort of inane banter they were used to, like 'your juices, baby', but even they realised that this phrase - or anything similar - was out of place at that moment. As out of place as they themselves were.

'Vodka?' their host suggested.

They both nodded. They were feeling so self-conscious that they didn't dare speak up and let their Siberian peasant accents show. But more than anything they were suspicious. They didn't trust so much hospitality from someone they had just met. There was a hidden agenda here and they wanted to know what it was.

After a curt nod from the man, the waitress left and later brought a tray with a bottle of the best Beluga vodka and three small glasses. She placed it all on the table and as she bent down, they could see that indeed, under her blouse, only her naked firm breasts were visible.

The host made the same brusque gesture and the girl disappeared. He filled the glasses.

'Here's to women and business,' he said, raising his glass.

The others followed suit and all three drank it in one gulp.

The vodka was excellent. Probably the best they had ever drunk.

Through the one-way window they watched as couples made their way to the private rooms in what looked like the prelude to a happy ending. The *'escorts'* - all of them stunning - looked as if they had been snatched from a beauty contest. There were plenty of girls with Eastern European features, tall and blonde with blue eyes, but there were also some brunettes who looked South American or Cuban or some such, and a few Asian girls. It seemed that, no matter what might be the sexual predilection of the gentlemen who visited *Irina la Dulce*, their tastes were provided for. And there they were, two former farm labourers, enjoying vodka and the sight of women they had only seen in the cinema and, what's more, for free. And on top of that, they were going to be offered a business proposition. Something didn't add up and they still didn't know what it was.

From that point on, their host started talking about himself, basically to big himself up. He endeavoured to impress them by telling them how he had progressed from a squalid suburb of Kiev to there. What he had had to do to get all that he had now and what he was willing to do not to lose it.

He didn't seem to have any interest in hearing what his new friends had to say on any subject. As he talked and talked, the glasses were refilled again and again and knocked back in one gulp. But one detail did not escape Vasili's attention. His new friend spoke in the plural, as if he represented someone, perhaps some group, or more likely, a company.

The two farmhands kept drinking and drinking the vodka and after the second bottle they were beginning to feel its effects, while their host seemed immune to the alcohol. When he thought they were sufficiently mellow, he got to the point.

'Well, gentlemen, let's talk business. Would you like to make some easy money?'

They might be a couple of peasant farm workers who had migrated there, but they knew all too well that making easy money was a false concept. However, they were willing to do anything to earn money, even if it was 'easy'.

'We want to earn money. If it's easy, all the better,' replied Vasili on behalf of both of them.

'Great! We need you to enter a house and take something.'

Although they were beginning to feel the effects of the dozen or so glasses of vodka that had slipped so easily down their throats, they still had a few functioning neurons left.

'You want us to commit a robbery.'

The man poured another round and as he drank his vodka, he replied.

'Well,' he said, shaking his head slightly, 'let's say it's a matter of retrieving something that shouldn't be where it is. It'll be a ten-minute job. No two ways about it. No risk involved. In and out. And five thousand euros each. But you must follow the instructions to the letter.'

They looked at each other and drank the latest shot their new friend had poured out. Five thousand euros! It had been a long time since they had seen that much money in one place. Grigori tried to remember the last time and remembered the bank heist in Sofia, with a couple of plastic guns. But that was a long time ago.

'What do we have to do?'

'Come back here in a week's time. Thursday. Not before midnight. If the doorman gives you any trouble, tell him I'm expecting you. Bring a passport photo. I'll give you your instructions then.'

'And if the guy asks us your name, what do we say?'

'Oleg. And your names are?'

'I'm Grigori.'

'And I'm Vasili.'

'Good. See you next Thursday then.'

As they got up to leave, they passed the blonde waitress who smiled at them with a half-professional, half-mocking look on her face.

'Thanks for coming. We look forward to seeing you again soon.'

'Thursday,' said Vasili, turning his head, just as she turned her back on him and walked towards the booth to retrieve the vodka bottles and glasses.

Once they had left the nightclub, they got into the car and looked for a place where they could have a last drink and compare thoughts. They soon found one, languishing in the middle of nowhere and barely visible, lit by a dim and flickering light that served to frighten off any doubtful customers. They sat down at a secluded table on the terrace and ordered two beers.

They waited for the waitress to bring them before they began to talk freely.

'What do you think?' Vasili asked. He had noticed that his friend was very quiet during the discussion at the club.

'It smells fishy to me, but what do you want me to say? You know as well as I do that we need the cash, and we need it as soon as possible. We're hardly in a position to pick and choose.'

'Yeah, but if we get caught...'

'Well, look on the bright side, Vasili.'

'Oh, you reckon there's a bright side?'

'If they catch us, we get a short spell in comfortable accommodation with three meals a day. And I don't think life is too bad in Spanish prisons. Certainly nothing compared to others we've been in.'

'You're right about that. But they won't deport us, will they? They won't send us back to Russia?'

'They don't do that here.'

'So, shall we go for it?'

'Let's drink to the deal. We're going to make five thousand euros really easily.'

'I don't think it'll be that easy. There's a catch here and I haven't worked out what it is yet.'

'Relax, Vasili. Just think about what you're going to do with all that money.'

'You're right. Let drink to the deal.'

***

As instructed, the following Thursday they showed up at the club in Puerto Banús. When they got there, before the bouncer could raise any objections, they said:

'Oleg is expecting us.'

The bouncer stepped aside and let them pass.

As they entered, they instinctively looked for the waitress, and when they spotted her, she motioned for them to follow her. She led them to the same private room as before, where Oleg was waiting for them. Before they sat down, Oleg signalled to the blonde and she made her way to the bar to serve the same drinks as last time to the boss and his guests. When she arrived with the bottle and glasses, they were again able to enjoy the view that was literally offered up in front of their eyes: the perfect breasts of the waitress as naked and as pert as ever, with their perfect proportions. At a gesture from Oleg, the girl remained in the room at a discreet distance.

He treats her like a dog, thought Vasili. With just a slight nod of the head she interprets and obeys.

'Let's drink to the success of our venture, gentlemen,' said Oleg, raising his glass and inviting the other two to do the same.

After finishing the first toast in one gulp, Oleg continued.

'In case there's any doubt, you still have time to pull out. If you decide to continue, I want to make it clear that no foolishness on your part will be tolerated. It would be regrettable and, believe me, tragic.'

The two friends got the message.

'No problem. We've made up our minds.'

'Good. The photos?'

'Yes, they're here.'

As they went to hand him the photos, instead of taking them, Oleg signalled to the waitress, who took them away.

'Don't worry. She'll be right back. I will now give you the information you need to do the job. Only the details you need to know. If you are not sure about anything, ask me. When Marina returns,' Oleg continued, 'she'll come back with two IDs used by a security company. You, then, are going to replace two security guards on a residential estate.'

'Are they ill?' Grigori asked.

'Something like that,' was Oleg's answer.

'How long are we going to be covering for them?'

'One night.'

The disappointment and utter bewilderment on the faces of both of them was clear to see. They were going to be paid five thousand euros for just one night's work?

'Excuse me,' Vasili interjected, 'If I understand you correctly, we're only going to work one night and we're going to be paid five thousand euros each. Is that what you're saying?'

'That's right. Exactly. I told you it would be easy money.'

'OK' said Vasili after letting out a long breath.

Next, Oleg explained the fine details of exactly what was expected of them.

'The day before the hit, a car will be delivered to you. You will use it to get to and from the residential complex. After you have received the money in exchange for the picture, you are to leave the car there, at the site of the rendezvous. So, you will have to take another car to the meeting place to drive away in. Is that all clear?'

And he went on.

'Here is a plan of the housing estate and its location in Marbella. It also shows the location of the house you are to break into. This other plan of the interior of the house indicates where the picture is, and there's a key to enter the house.

It's essential that you follow these instructions on how to protect it, how to wrap it and how to ensure that it is not damaged. That is really important. If the buyer were to reject it because of damage, you would be held responsible and believe me, you don't want that to happen.

When you get to the security checkpoint you have to give the names that correspond to the ID cards. The signatures don't matter much. Nobody really checks them.

You must enter the house precisely fifteen minutes before the end of your patrol. After that, you sign out, leave the security van for the next guard and leave the scene. You go directly to the appointed meeting place to make the exchange. That information will be given to you 24 hours before the day of the operation.'

And to finish off, he gave them one final important instruction:

'Once you deliver the picture and receive the money, we will never see each other again. I don't want to see you turning up here. Oh, and you can forget about Marina, even in your dreams.'

That was the hardest part of the deal, especially for Vasili.

'Any questions, anything you're not sure about?' Oleg prompted.

'What about security systems? Alarms, cameras, dogs...' Grigori asked.

'You don't need to worry. We'll take care of all that.'

This "we" worried them. They didn't know how to interpret it. They weren't sure if it was something that provided security or some sort of stability, or if, on the contrary, it represented a threat to them.

'I have another question,' Vasili said.

'Go on'

'If you have all the information and the resources, why don't you, whoever you are, do it yourselves?'

'Good question. It deserves a straight answer. A large number of highly competent people have been involved in this job. Each is an expert in his or her field, but none knows the name of any of the others. It's called watertight compartmentalization and guarantees confidentiality. We have to preserve the identity of certain very important people who should not, cannot, be involved in something like this.'

'But we've met you and we know your name is Oleg,' said Grigori, letting his big mouth get the better of him.

'Is that something I should be concerned about?' growled Oleg menacingly, sitting up in his seat and looking hostile.

'No, no, no. I'm very sorry, sir. My friend has expressed himself badly. What he meant to say,' he said, shooting a withering look at his companion, 'is that it seems like a contradiction. That's all. You needn't worry at all. I assure you.'

'There is absolutely no contradiction. I have already told you that we will never see each other again. And that better be the case, because if not, as I said before, the consequences would be tragic. For you, of course.'

'We've got the message, sir.' Vasili replied. 'Don't worry, really.

We have no intention of complicating things. Get in, get out, get paid and adios. You've made it crystal clear.'

'I hope so.'

At that moment, Marina returned.

'Here are the two ID cards and two bags. Inside are the uniforms you have to wear.'

'What if they don't fit?' Grigori asked

'They'll fit; they are your size. We've already checked,' Oleg replied.

'How?' Vasili asked, amazed and at the same time a little alarmed.

'By going into your houses and opening the wardrobe,' Oleg answered with a smile on his lips.

The answer chilled them to the bone. They turned so pale they looked like two corpses, and it was clear, if they didn't watch out, that's what they'd be in the not-too-distant future. It was then that they realised that there was indeed no such thing as 'easy money'. But there was no turning back now.

'Before you go, I want to offer you a gesture of goodwill to show our confidence in you.'

He's still speaking in the plural, Vasili reflected.

'Here's half the money up front,' and he handed them each an envelope with two thousand five hundred euros in it. 'I hope you get a lot of pleasure out of it. Good night, gentlemen, and I don't wish to ever see you again,' Oleg concluded.

'Goodbye,' said Vasili. 'And thank you.'

Before they got up to leave, they drank the last few dregs of vodka. They savoured it as if it were the last they would ever have. When they got up, their legs were shaking, they were ashen-faced and they were beginning to think that their lives were in serious danger. So much so that, as they left, they didn't even dare to look at Marina when she said goodbye to them.

'Good night, gentlemen.'

On this occasion, she didn't add her favourite phrase 'we hope to see you here again soon', which was very significant.

They left the club carrying the bags and went straight to the car. Both remained in complete silence, staring blankly ahead, for several minutes. Finally, Vasili, who always took the lead, said:

'Grigori.'

'Yes?'

'I don't want that vodka to be the last I ever have. Let's get drunk with some of the money they just gave us.'

'I'm with you all the way on that, but first, give me a moment.'

Grigori got out of the car and walked towards the sea, where the yachts were moored. Before he had got very far, he threw up.

Returning to the car, he said to his friend:

'Whenever you like. I'm ready now.'

And they headed off to find a classy joint where they could use the two and a half thousand euros they had in their pockets. They were not at all sure that they would get to enjoy the rest.

Then one day they received a call which summoned them to the parking lot of a shopping centre in Marbella. There they were given the car they were to use for the job and they were told the location where they would exchange the picture for the remaining money. A quiet and secluded area where they could perform the operation undisturbed.

Once they had the car, they drove to the site of the handover and left their Audi there. That would be the one they would use to leave the scene.

Suddenly, the voice of Grigori, who was dozing in the seat next to him, shook Vasili out of his thoughts.

'What are you thinking about, Vasili? You've been as quiet as a ghost for a while now. I can see you've calmed down at last.'

'Well, I was just going over how we got into this mess. Everything that's happened to us in the last two weeks.'

'Well, in the end everything turned out all right. We got the job done, we got paid and we're still alive.'

'Yeah.'

'But there's still something that's bugging you, isn't there?'

'Yes, there is. I've been driving all this time and I still don't know where we're going.'

'Are you okay, d'you want me to drive for a while?'

'No, no, I'm fine. Besides, driving relaxes me.'

'When the sun comes up, which won't be long, we'll find a place to fuel up and have breakfast, okay?'

'That's a good idea. I'm starving.'

3. The theft is discovered

Aaron Bukowski's personal jet landed at Malaga's international airport, in the zone reserved for private aircraft. His chauffeur was waiting for him there, with one of the finest cars in his impressive fleet, a Rolls Royce Phantom.

As he left the plane, he said goodbye as usual to the crew, which consisted of the captain, the first officer, a stewardess and a relief pilot.

'Did you have a comfortable flight, sir?' the captain asked.

'Splendid, Captain. I even managed a little snooze. Thank you very much. You're all very helpful,' he said, turning his head to look at each one of the crew members. 'I don't have any plans to fly again soon, so, if you wish, you can take a break until further notice.'

'Thank you very much, sir. You're very kind. Whenever you need us, just let us know, we're always pleased to be of service,' replied the captain.

Bukowski was an immensely wealthy man, which never prevented him from treating all the people he encountered with a respect and appreciation that was reciprocated by everyone who knew him. His employees felt a genuine and true devotion for the old man, who, in spite of his advanced age, still maintained his mental faculties at full capacity and showed great dedication to his work. Only a certain difficulty in moving around and a few minor ailments typical of his age gave away his advancing years.

The stewardess had, as usual, already collected the minimal luggage he was in the habit of travelling with. As he settled himself into the vehicle, she placed it in the car's capacious boot. The chauffeur thanked her and gently closed the tailgate, then returned to the driver's seat.

Looking through the driver's rear-view mirror, the chauffeur inquired:

'Did you have a good flight, sir?'

'Excellent.'

'And was the trip a success?'

'Yes, Dimas, it was. Thanks for asking.'

'Home, sir, or would you prefer...?'

'Home, please. I'm a little tired. This change of time zones is going to be the death of me.'

'Make yourself comfortable, sir, and might I suggest you take a nap?'

'Thank you. I think I'll take your advice.'

'Is the air conditioning okay or should I turn it down?'

'A little cooler, please.'

'Very well, sir. If you change your mind and get cold, please let me know.'

'I will.'

They left the airport and headed for Marbella on the dual carriageway. Unsurprisingly, Bukowski fell asleep on the way. Observing him through the rear-view mirror, Dimas thought he looked exhausted.

They arrived at the house just as Bukowski was waking up. Dimas drove up to the main entrance, where the butler, Tomas, came out to meet them. He opened the door for his employer to step out and greeted him.

'Welcome, sir, how are you feeling today after your journey?'

'Fine, thanks, Tomas. Perhaps a little more tired than at other times. I think it's the weather in London. Too humid, too hot or too cold. I don't know. That river is bad for my health,' he joked as he made his way rather stiffly to the entrance.

'Next time, we'll have the river drained for you, sir,' Thomas joked, which brought a smile to Bukowski's face.

Meanwhile, Dimas had given the luggage to the housekeeper, Guadalupe, who, after greeting her employer, had carried it upstairs to the master bedroom.

Bukowski would use the lift. But first he wanted to go to his office, on the first floor, to check his post and his emails.

Tomas, who was not only a butler but also his personal valet, turned to Guadalupe:

'Thanks very much, Guadalupe. Don't worry. I'll take care of the unpacking.'

It was then that they heard a loud cry of distress from their master in the study on the floor below. Both Tomas and Guadalupe ran downstairs as fast as they could, to see what had happened. When they entered the office, they saw him with his head sunk in his hands, sobbing like a child. It was heartbreaking to see him like that. They were at a loss to understand what had happened. He had seemed fine when he arrived.

And then suddenly Tomas looked at the wall and realized. His eyes widened in pure horror, as if he had seen a ghost, but he signalled Guadalupe not to say anything. She still did not understand.

'Sir, are you all right?'

'I've been robbed, Tomas. They've stolen it from me. Again! They've stolen it again!'

Guadalupe then noticed that there was a blank space on the wall. She never knew how to value what hung on the walls, but from her employer's reaction, it must have been valuable. She was aghast and had turned pale.

'Sir. We must call the police immediately,' Tomas suggested.

Bukowski, still holding his head in his hands, seemed not to have heard his butler.

'Sir?'

'I'm fine, Tomas. Yes, we must call the police, but before that, please locate Daniel Olavarría in my address book. Call him and ask him to come as soon as possible.'

'Before the police, sir?'

'Yes, please.'

'Fine, sir, as you wish.'

Aaron Bukowski had slumped against the back of his chair. He was breathing heavily and his head was leaning against the backrest with his eyes closed. Then he opened his eyes, got up from his seat and went to the globe drinks cabinet in his office. He opened it and took out a bottle of whisky and a tumbler. He poured himself a shot and downed it in one gulp. The warmth of the alcohol going down his throat made him feel a little better. It calmed him down. He poured himself another, a little more generous, and decided he would savour it while he waited for Daniel Olavarría to arrive.

4. Ivan Orlov

Barely thirty minutes after the robbery, the picture arrived at the yacht *Irina*, moored in Puerto Banús.

The vessel was sailing under the flag of the Cayman Islands, although it officially belonged to a Ukrainian company, so it was also flying the Ukrainian flag, as required. In reality, the only individual using the boat was Ivan Orlov.

Ivan Orlov, known in certain circles as "The Russian", was - at least in theory – the Ukrainian consul in Monaco. When his multifarious engagements allowed him to, he divided his free time between the principality and Marbella.

He was a man of normal height and build, in his late seventies, though he didn't look it.

He was one of the most powerful men on the planet. His power rested on two pillars: he was a personal friend of the supreme authority in Russia, President Igor Ruskin, and he was also the most important FSB - formerly KGB - agent. He could practically be said to be acting under the direct orders of his friend Igor, which put the head of Russian espionage, his theoretical boss, in a difficult position. His arrogant behaviour was probably due to this close relationship, which gave him a quasi-untouchable status.

Born in St. Petersburg, he showed early signs of above-average intelligence. After high school, he went to St. Petersburg University where he studied at the Graduate School of Management. After excelling in his university studies, he was contacted by the KGB and began to work for them. He was sent to the then East Germany, specifically to Dresden. There, he soon became friendly with a young man who, like him, was taking his first steps in the KGB. His name was Igor Ruskin. Their rising careers within the KGB and the state organisation ran parallel to each other.

The post of Ukrainian consul in Monaco, in addition to providing him with diplomatic status, served as a cover for his many activities, most of which were of dubious - and sometimes not so dubious - legality. In fact, everyone assumed that he was prepared to deal in anything that made money, be it drugs, arms or stolen works of art.

When he needed to get around quickly, he used a private jet. The yacht was another business tool he used for his escapades, to amuse himself or to entertain guests, and on occasions like this one, he simply used it as a taxi.

It was very important for this operation that he was not seen with the stolen picture anywhere in public, not even on the yacht. It was the best way to prevent him from being linked to the theft of the artwork. Therefore, the yacht and the crew - who, of course, knew nothing about it - would simply take the package from Marbella to Monte Carlo, while he was thousands of miles away. He would arrive in the capital of Monaco by air, in his jet, on the agreed date. That was the plan, as he reminded his chief of security when he called from Marbella to announce that he had the package in his possession.

Yuri Maslanka, Ivan Orlov's security chief, was fifty-two years old. He was Orlov's right-hand man and his life was in his hands. He alone, and no one else, could have been entrusted with the transfer of the stolen artwork. Yuri was a Russian secret service agent like his boss. He came from a family with a long military tradition and held the rank of lieutenant colonel. He ruled his men with an iron discipline and his behaviour was completely predictable. When necessary, he could be as cold as ice, both in analysing a situation and in executing his decisions. He never lost his cool and was always one step ahead of the pack. His loyalty to Ivan was unquestionable, and he harboured the hope that he himself would someday benefit from his boss's closeness to the president.

From the first moment, Ivan realised the importance of this mission, despite the fact that even he was being kept in the dark about some of the details. He knew that, but he did not want to embarrass his friend the president. In addition to friendship, there was loyalty.

The meeting at which he received his orders was held in the president's office in the Kremlin. The only people present were Igor, the head of the FSB and Ivan himself. No unnecessary loose ends, they insisted. Afterwards, when he arrived in Monaco, he was to contact an Arab millionaire who, he was told, belonged to the family of the Emir of Qatar. The meeting was to take place at the Emir's palace in the Principality.

***

Once the crew of the *Irina* was ready and in place, the yacht's captain began to give the instructions to depart from dock, repeated by the first mate:

> 'Standby to cast off. Cast off port bow line. Rudder to starboard. Cast off stern bow line. Idle away.'

The yacht set sail from Puerto Banús for Monaco.

5. Bukowski and the picture

Bukowski prepared to wait patiently in his office for the arrival of Daniel Olavarría. He was trying to calm his breathing and, above all, his heart rate, which had shot up, and that was not good for his already ailing heart. The whisky he was enjoying had not been prescribed by the doctor either, but at that moment, it was the best medicine he had available to him.

As he sat there, alone, exhausted, dejected, Tomas waited by the door in case anything should happen to his master or he might need some refreshment. The rest of the staff were upset about what had happened, but Tomas had given instructions not to disturb him. They should all keep well away.

At that moment, Aaron was recalling memories that he had tucked away in a corner, in the depths of his soul, that he would never be able to forget. It was as though the ghost that had been haunting him since he was a child had risen once again from its grave. He retraced the history of that picture and the various misfortunes that had befallen it and the different people that had owned it. That masterpiece contained within its frame not only something of incalculable value but also a part of the very history of his family and of the *Shoah*.

The picture was a self-portrait drawn in charcoal, attributed to Albrecht Dürer, from his early years. It appeared to be an early exercise in craftsmanship by what was later to be an accomplished master. According to the information he had, his great-grandfather, an antiquarian, bought it from a Polish gypsy, a traveller who sold scrap metal and anything else he considered useless. After buying it for a few eslotis, - small change that would allow the itinerant to eat well and, more importantly, to drink well

– Aaron's great-grandfather had the drawing analysed by a more experienced colleague. When the provenance of the work was confirmed, it was looked after with the care and respect it deserved.

Then, with the invasion of Poland by the Nazis, came the looting of all works of art, especially those belonging to Jews. The Nazis showed a voracious, virtually insatiable, appetite when it came to appropriating anything of value. Their strategy was basically to offer a derisory purchase price for a work of art or other item that was not even for sale. In exchange for the paltry sum offered, the owner was led to believe that he would not be sent to a concentration camp if he agreed to sign the documents for the forced sale. The idea was to give the appearance of a legal sale when in reality it was extortion. Of course, they had no choice but to accept the offer, but on occasions, and there were many, in addition to being compelled to undersell their property, they were still sent to concentration camps, from which they never emerged.

And this was the case for his family. His entire family, like so many others, were confined in the Warsaw ghetto. Later, his grandparents and parents were sent to the Treblinka concentration camp, where they died. Aaron only managed to survive thanks to his saving angel in the form of a woman named Irena Sendler. She risked her life to save the lives of thousands of children who, like him, would have died had it not been for her courage and imagination. She smuggled them out of the ghetto hidden in crates, ambulances, coffins or even, once, in a consignment of bricks, and if they were babies, she drugged them just enough to stop them making any noise.

After the war, Bukowski found himself completely alone in a shattered world. He tried to overcome the pain, fear and bitterness. He decided to settle down, make something of himself and continue his ancestors' business: diamonds, jewellery and antiques. Perpetuating the family legacy was the least he could do for them, to honour their memory.

Many years after the war, when he had reached an impressive level of prosperity through hard work, talent and sacrifice, he began to search for this looted work of art. It was the last object of value that the Nazis took from his family, since when they returned for more there was nothing left to take. That is why they were confined to the ghetto and then to Treblinka. In a way, that drawing represented the last breath of his loved ones, the last link to a life of semi-freedom before the final condemnation, and he had to get it back no matter what the cost.

The undertaking was not an easy one. You don't find a work plundered by the Nazis hanging in an exhibition in a gallery. A lot of research had to be done in historical documents, libraries and government departments. It involved knocking on many doors and often obliged him to have dealings with people with little or no humanity or compassion. After years of fruitless searching, travelling halfway across Europe, advertising in the press, consulting with expert colleagues and, on occasion, with thieves and dealers of stolen art, he managed to find the new owner. It was not easy to get the individual to agree to meet him. It was like admitting that he had an object that, by all rights, should not belong to him. But Aaron Bukowski was a born businessman, a man who understood human weakness and was well aware of the depths to which human beings could sink. Nothing could shock him anymore.

In this way, he discovered that an individual called Hans Joseph Kauffmann was the son of a Nazi diplomat who fled after the war and took refuge in Spain, in Alicante. To be precise, in a town called Denia.

The meeting was not an easy one, emotionally speaking, although it took place in an atmosphere of impeccable politeness. Aaron, very subtly, slipped in the idea of how they had been forced to sell the picture, in the hope of rekindling, if only minimally, any smouldering embers of a sense of guilt on the part of its current owner. The discussion began to turn in Aaron's favour when he suggested a certain amount of money as 'compensation' for the inconvenience, on the grounds that it was a family memento. Eventually, a financial settlement was reached and Aaron Bukowski bought back the masterpiece that had belonged to his family.

And now, once again, they had stolen the drawing from him. The Dürer self-portrait was gone again, but now he no longer had the same energy as before. He had more money than then, but he was already an old man with the normal afflictions of his age and did not have the strength to carry out the enormous task of finding out who had stolen it and how much they were going to demand for its return. He was determined to call in a specialist in recovering stolen works of art. So he instructed his butler to contact the only man he could trust with the task: Daniel Olavarría.

6. Daniel Olavarría and Bukowski

Daniel Olavarría, a native of Donostia-San Sebastian, was considered a veritable superstar in the art world, both when it came to recommending the purchase of artwork to his clients, and when it came to examining and researching a possible forgery or a scam. But where he excelled beyond all others was when it came to recovering stolen works of art. In this he was the very best investigator of art crime in Europe.

He studied Art History at university in Granada. It was there that he fell in love with Andalusia and discovered an immense artistic heritage that was largely unprotected. As a result, to begin with his dealings were of a somewhat unscrupulous nature and for a short period of time, he devoted himself more to plundering undiscovered sites (Iberian and Phoenician, above all), rather than providing the care and protection that these jewels of antiquity demanded. To the extent that he almost got into serious trouble with the authorities.

But at the same time, he was able to win the trust and friendship of certain professional thieves, which served him well in his later profession. Even in hell you had to have friends, and he followed that principle literally. For this reason, he still maintained excellent relations with people in the criminal world, where, despite the fact that everyone knew what he did and who he worked with, he was respected. He always kept his agreements with them. He was always reliable.

He now lived in Marbella, not far from where Aaron Bukowski had his residence. And how did a Basque from San Sebastian end up living in Marbella? There were several reasons for such a decision. There was a time when leaving his homeland was a matter of life and death, as it was for so many others. Some had the opportunity to do so and others did not.

So, forced to go through the ordeal of having to leave his family home, he tried to find a new one, as far away as possible from that murderous conflict. In time, he also discovered that the food was not so bad in those latitudes. He remembered his good times at the university in Granada and decided to migrate to that area, although he chose Marbella.

He soon fell in love with the way of life in Marbella; the climate, the people, the parties and the beach clubs, and not only because of the women who frequented these places of entertainment. Socialising in these establishments allowed him to mix in the most select circles on the Costa del Sol, get to know some of the most important people, find out what they did for a living and what they spent their money on. It was always good to be where the money moved, and in Marbella it moved a lot. Moreover, many of the owners of these businesses ended up becoming his personal friends and clients and trusted him to advise them on how to invest in art legitimately. His highly confidential list of contacts included prestigious businessmen, aristocrats, bankers, politicians and world-class gourmet chefs.

He lived alone in a luxury private estate, with round-the-clock surveillance, surrounded by mostly foreign neighbours. His work and his constant travelling over the years had not allowed him to form a traditional family, something which now, in his late fifties, he was beginning to miss. It was not easy to find a woman willing to spend long periods of time alone while her husband travelled the world chasing shadows to recover works of art, some of which no one had ever heard of. That was another reason why he was beginning to think about getting away from all that hustle and bustle, working a little less, taking on fewer commissions, enjoying the money he had earned through honest toil and, if possible, finding a partner. He didn't want children, so he was looking for a woman over forty and with her biological clock stopped for good. And it wasn't easy either. She had to be cultured, educated, classy, speak several languages and, of course, attractive. And any woman like that, meeting all these conditions, was probably already taken.

He kept fit by jogging early in the mornings or playing paddle tennis with neighbours and friends on the courts of the residential complex. At six foot five, his healthy lifestyle gave him a physique that would appeal to any woman. His culture, his knowledge of art, the fact that he spoke several languages, his wealth and his equanimity, undoubtedly helped him on many occasions to cope more easily with loneliness.

Every day he used to go down to the café on the private estate to have breakfast and read the newspapers, using his laptop to connect to the internet. It was a way of getting out of his retreat without straying too far, while enjoying the peaceful surroundings, the gardens, the weather that was almost always sunny and warm and the music that was playing to entertain the café's mainly foreign customers.

The waiter, Fernando seemed to be permanently present and never seemed to go off duty. He knew his habitual order: coffee with warm milk and saccharine, and toast with butter and strawberry jam.

He was immersed in this well-established routine, reading the news on his computer, when his mobile rang. It was an unknown number. Something unexpected is about to be sprung on me, he thought, before answering the phone.

'Yes?'

'Mr Olavarría?'

'Yes, how can I help you?'

'Sir, I'm calling on behalf of Mr Bukowski, Aaron Bukowski. The gentleman asks you to stop by his house at your earliest convenience. He has an important assignment for you.'

This was a member of staff calling on someone's behalf and using the word "sir". He already had some idea of the type of client. Besides, the surname rang a bell.

'Can you tell me what this is about?'

'I'm sorry, sir, but I'm not authorised to reveal that information and certainly not over the phone, but I can tell you that he has had many excellent testimonials of your previous work and would like your help.'

It was a very subtle way of making it clear what he was needed for.

'If you give me the address I can be there in less than an hour.'

Daniel made sure he had enough time to research the name he had just been given. He didn't intend to go to an unfamiliar address, to a man he knew nothing about, to discuss a matter he had not been briefed on, even though he had a pretty good idea of what it was about.

Although he found some information by browsing the internet, in reality there was very little detail on the man. But it was enough to make him no longer a perfect stranger.

Aaron Bukowski was a wealthy businessman, with interests in diverse sectors in various capitals around the world. He also held a significant number of shares in companies that owned luxury hotels, exclusive restaurants, high-end boutiques and so on. In addition, he was the owner of one of the world's most expensive chain of jeweller's shops, scattered all over the world from London, Paris and New York to Dubai and Hong Kong. He was immensely rich and enjoyed buying works of art. That was why the name Bukowski rang a bell.

He didn't need to enter the directions he had been given into the car's

GPS. He knew how to get there. One of his friends also had a villa on the same estate.

When he reached the security post at the entrance, the guard took note of the number plate, his name and who he was going to visit, after which he told him which way to go.

From the outside, the house was not particularly sumptuous or eye-catching. It was a two-storey building with large, manicured gardens, leafy trees and a pebbled path leading to the main entrance.

He got out of the car and climbed the four steps to the door. Before he could ring the bell, the door opened. It was obvious that they were waiting for him and had been following his approach since he had entered the grounds.

'Good morning. I believe Mr Bukowski is expecting me.'

'Good morning, Mr Olavarría. Be so good as to come with me please, this way.'

The voice of the man who greeted him was the same as the one on the phone. That accent, that intonation and those formal manners were unmistakable.

Tomas the butler, led him through to the study where Aaron normally attended to his business and received visitors. It was situated to the right of the entrance and its windows faced the main façade, so that from his desk he could always tell who was approaching the front door.

On the wood-panelled walls hung a number of paintings, which Daniel immediately identified. He also made a rough estimate of their value. On the far wall, just behind the chair of the man who had summoned him, there was an empty space. He saw it when the man moved his chair to stand up and greet him.

'Mr Bukowski?'

'Mr Olavarría, I can't thank you enough for responding to my request in such a prompt manner. I'm very sorry to put you to this trouble and I apologise for it, but I'm very anxious and extremely agitated, which is not at all good for my heart.'

'Don't worry on my account, Mr Bukowski. Tell me what it is that you're so anxious and upset about that couldn't be spoken about on the phone. How can I help you? What's happened?'

'Before we get down to business, would you like a drink, a coffee or perhaps something stronger?'

'Coffee would be fine.'

'Nothing for me, Tomas.'

Tomas disappeared through the door to organise this and a maid arrived from the kitchen carrying a hand wrought silver tray with coffee and Danish pastries.

Whereupon Aaron Bukowski explained in detail who the author of the self-portrait was, how he had discovered the theft, the history of the picture, what it meant to him, and how worried he was that, feeling so old and somewhat ill, he would not have time to return the work of art to its rightful owner. Besides, he had no heirs and didn't want to leave this world without recovering the picture.

Daniel listened carefully to the explanation and began to realise that his plan to withdraw from this kind of work was going to be more complicated than he had thought. He couldn't refuse the old man's request and it was not because he needed the money. The story he had related touched him to the heart. An immensely wealthy man, he had no relatives to bequeath his fortune to and his only aim, in what remained of his life, was to recover something that had been stolen from him for the second time and to leave this world at peace with himself and his murdered loved ones.

After listening to his prospective client, Daniel began to ask him a series of questions related to the burglary: Had he called the police? How come there was no one in the house? How did the burglars get in? Why weren't the alarms turned on? Did he trust the staff? Had any strangers visited the house recently?

'Regarding the question of whether I have had visitors that I didn't know, Mr Olavarría, I must tell you that I often host dinners at my house for eminent people from very different spheres. Arab millionaires, politicians, renowned businessmen, artists, writers, philosophers, ambassadors, gallery owners... I have no family and I like to surround myself with cultured people, with intelligent and pleasant conversation. I encourage encounters between unknown artists and collectors who are interested in investing and sometimes go on to serve as patrons. So, yes, I'm afraid that many different people have come into this house. If you're thinking of asking me for a list, I might as well give you the phone directory.'

'I see,' said Daniel laconically. 'I don't suppose you suspect anyone in particular.'

'I have no idea. I'm sure you understand, don't you?'

Daniel nodded his head, showing his feelings with a shrug of frustration.

At the end of the questioning, Aaron made the situation very clear:

'Mr Olavarría, I have heard excellent reports about you, your integrity and your competence. I have confidence in you and your expertise, and of course, there's no limit on the budget to recover the picture. Whether you succeed or not, you will be rewarded for your work.'

'Thank you for your words and your confidence, Mr Bukowski,

and believe me, if I accept this commission, it's not for the money.'

'I know that. I've been informed on that point too.'

'But before I commit myself to accept the assignment, I have to study the chances of success. It's very generous of you to promise a payment even in the event of failure, but that is not how I work. I would first like to have certain guarantees that this will not be the case, that I can indeed help to recover the artwork. And for that I need to analyse the situation and devise a plan of action, give myself some sort of road map. I need a few days to think about it.'

'Take as long as necessary, but remember that for me, time is running out.'

'Anyway, the first thing we must do is call the police.'

7. Daniel Olavarría and his musings

I'm afraid my hopes to find peace and quiet in retirement will have to wait for a while. This was not in my plans and, what's worse, I could be faced with a proposition like this at any time. I have to establish a red line beyond which I say no. But in this case, it's a matter of conscience. I can't let him down. The poor man has suffered so much in his life! It was dreadful enough that he lost his whole family at the hands of the Nazis, but in addition, all the works of art that they possessed were stolen. And now it has happened for a second time. It seems like a curse of fate! The man is aware that he doesn't have long to live, maybe only a few years, and he wants to leave this earth with a clear conscience, having fulfilled his obligation to recover what's rightfully his. I can't turn my back on him.

Now, let's see where to start unravelling the threads of this case. This is not the work of a couple of petty criminals. There's a lot of prior preparation and background knowledge here. Based on what I've been told, it all appears to be extremely professional. The burglars took advantage of the one day when there was no one looking after the house. The alarms didn't go off and the security cameras weren't switched on. To enter a house with this level of protection, in an exclusive estate like this, without attracting attention or breaking a pane of glass and being able to disable all the security systems, that's not something that just anyone can do. What's more, no other paintings have been taken. This drawing attributed to Dürer is the only one, but I have seen others of equal or even greater value hanging on the walls of his office and on the staircase leading to the first floor.

All this tells me that the thieves had a high level of detailed information and were well prepared. I'm beginning to suspect that they had help from a member of the household staff. What I don't understand is why they only took that one drawing. Was it some kind of payback? Was it a competitor or collector? Did the individual he had bought it back from want to pull the same trick twice and so had arranged for it to be stolen again? I doubt it. Too much risk and too much investment in resources. How many people were involved in this?

I've got too many questions and no answers. But it seems to me that I already have an answer: I accept the case. I don't know where on earth to start, but I can't abandon him. One thing's for sure, though: If I wanted to, I could charge a small fortune for the job. But I won't be doing it for the money.

For the moment, I will go to Alhaurín tomorrow to see my mate Stefano di Bari. See if he knows anything. I'll take him some cigarettes, that always puts him in a good mood.

8. The police begin their investigation

Once the call had been made from Bukowski's house, the police arrived almost immediately. It was a full-scale response. At least, thought Bukowski, they had turned up in unmarked cars and without the sirens blaring. Otherwise, the swarm of cars at the entrance to his property would have attracted the press who were always hovering around like carrion birds.

Three cars and a white van with no windows and no lettering on the sides arrived. They could have been painters, decorators or bricklayers. In the van, they had a whole mobile laboratory for analysis and corroboration of evidence. One of the cars was occupied by Lieutenant Eduardo Navarro and in the rest were all the crime scene investigators.

When they arrived at the villa, they left the cars at the top of the driveway, safe from the prying eyes of those who might be watching from other houses or from the street.

At the head of the parade was Superintendent Frutos, chief of the Marbella police station. He only showed up on special occasions, and this was one of them. It was not a spectacle that would go unnoticed, especially given the white jumpsuits that the investigators had to wear to avoid contaminating the crime scene.

They made their way up the stairs leading to the main entrance. There was no need to ring the bell. Tomas, the butler, was waiting and opened the door for them immediately.

'Chief Superintendent Frutos, from the police. These men are with me,' he said, showing his badge.

'Please, follow me.'

'Navarro, you come with me. Have your team take statements from all the staff and get the forensic team to process the house,' he said before following in the butler's footsteps.

Bukowski was sitting in the lounge, in front of a huge fireplace that looked as though on a cold winter's night, it would do a fine job of heating that immense space.

Jesús Frutos was a police officer with extensive professional experience. He didn't have long to wait before retirement. He was from the old school, the kind where you started from the bottom and, through hard work and long hours, worked your way up step by step. He was a tough character.

He had been divorced several times. For many people, it wasn't easy to combine family and police work. Despite the financial support he was obliged to pay to his ex-wives, he owned a villa, with a hefty mortgage. The house was never very tidy or clean, a task he had entrusted to Lara, a Russian girl whom he employed as a cleaner. His extensive outlays did not prevent him from enjoying worldly pleasures, such as alcohol and women, something that aroused more than a little envy and some misgivings amongst his colleagues. He used to say - with a certain joviality that was not without regret - that in the end, whores were cheaper.

He had never been known for being the life and soul of a party, but his personal circumstances had managed to sour his already sullen character even more. Sparing with words and even more so with gestures, no one could ever guess what was going through his mind, whether he was investigating a case or playing poker, which, by the way, he didn't always win. He did not give the impression of someone that was likely to suffer an attack of anxiety.

He was one of the most experienced members of the force and he knew

- or rather sensed - that he had been assigned this job as a lead-up to his retirement. He accepted that this would come sooner rather than later and that unless a straight flush or a lucky night at the Casino were to help him, his enviable financial situation would not last long once he retired because his pension would be a mere pittance.

Several young people had been included in the team under his command, in an attempt to modernise his somewhat old-fashioned methods. His superiors also hoped that he would pass on his undoubted experience and teach them what you can't learn from a book: a policeman's nose for the job.

The new recruits were very well qualified. They had high level academic degrees and were experts in IT and the use of social networks, something that for him had come too late and he had absolutely no interest in learning about.

For this case, the investigation would be led by his inspector, Eduardo Navarro, a young, intelligent man with a bright future in the police. Navarro had a degree in criminology and a master's degree in cybercrime. He was what Frutos himself described as a "chip off the new block".

'Mr Bukowski,' said Frutos, proffering his hand to the victim of the crime, 'I sincerely regret that we meet up again in such circumstances.'

'Yes, so do I. Last time was much more pleasant.'

'It was indeed. It was a delicious dinner and most stimulating company.'

'We will repeat it and celebrate the successful outcome of this incident.'

'I shall be delighted. I assure you.'

'Please be seated. Would you like something to drink?'

'No, thanks, I'm fine.'

'A little water, perhaps?'

'Yes please, that would be nice'

'Excuse me, Superintendent, do you two already know each other?' Navarro asked discreetly.

'Yes, we do. I have had the pleasure of being invited by Mr Bukowski on a couple of occasions to some of his magnificent soirées, notable both for the quality of the food and the quality of the guests... except for me, of course.'

'You're very modest, Jesús,' Bukowski intervened as he motioned to Tomas, who withdrew to the kitchen to return a few minutes later with some glasses and bottles of water on a silver tray. It sounded strange to Navarro to hear his boss, a chief superintendent, being called by his first name.

Bukowski was patient with the intense questioning that Frutos and Navarro put him through, very similar to the one Daniel Olavarría had previously carried out. While this was going on, the rest of the team, the crime scene investigators, swept Bukowski's villa for more than four hours collecting evidence, taking statements and personal data and fingerprints from all of the staff, and photographing every corner of the house.

When, at last, they all left, Bukowski said to the butler:

'Tomas, I'm going to bed. I'm exhausted. It's been a terrible day. I was already quite tired from the trip to London, but all this is too much for me. Please make sure no one disturbs me.'

As they left the house, Frutos made as if to return to the police station and Navarro suggested - not without some astonishment - that "maybe it would be a good idea to pay a visit to the security guards." Frutos nodded as if to imply a momentary lapse of attention, and the two set off for the security checkpoint at the entrance to the residential estate. They needed to talk to the people responsible, get their fingerprints, check the shifts, find out the names of all of them and where they were that night and what they knew or had seen. They also needed the security footage. The guards who should have been there the night before were off duty and were thought to be at home. They were sent for, while Navarro and his men continued to question their colleagues.

Before returning to the police station, Navarro asked:

'Do we know any more about the guards from last night?'

'Not yet.'

'Keep on it. Do you have their home addresses?'

'Yes, we do. Here you go.'

'We're going back to the station. If you haven't contacted them within an hour, call me, as a matter of priority, at the station. OK?'

'Yes sir, I will.'

At the end of that first foray, Navarro organised a pooling of information in the briefing room at the police station. Superintendent Frutos also attended the meeting.

Frutos opened up the discussion in the same way he always kicked off an investigation: by examining the working hypotheses.

'What have we got?'

'They only took one piece of art, but there were many more pictures on the walls, some of them certainly more valuable,' Navarro pointed out.

'A contract job?'

'I reckon so,' replied Navarro.

'We don't know anything about a possible ransom either, do we?'

'Not at the moment, no. But they might have been hired by a collector...'

'Is this the only house that has been burgled?'

'It looks like it, so far at least, we have no news of anything else.'

'OK, continue.'

'Also, they didn't break any windows, or force any doors to get in.'

'They entered with a key, Superintendent,' confirmed the head of the CSI team, who had been examining the various possible points of entry.

'Any suspicion of complicity among the staff?' asked Frutos.

'We need to check their alibis and their details: emails, social networks, bank accounts, mobiles, etc.'

'Alarms, security cameras?' Frutos followed the steps in order.

'The cameras were deactivated and so were all other security measures. This wasn't done by a couple of amateurs, Superintendent.'

'It takes a skilled expert to pull that off, sir,' commented the electronics specialist who had been analysing the failure of the security systems. 'This isn't something that just anyone can do.'

'Right. So we have the theft of a single work of art. They entered using a key and there's no footage from inside the house and the alarms didn't go off. Surveillance cameras from the security company, from the surrounding area?'

'We've requested them and still need to look at them. Maybe they'll give us some leads. Also, the security company is trying to track down the men who did the shift last night,' said Navarro.

'So why the delay?'

'Well, apparently they can't get hold of them. They could be sleeping or have gone to the beach.'

Frutos made that face he used to make when he played cards. The one that nobody knew how to interpret, but it looked like he was mulling over something that Navarro hadn't thought of yet.

'I told them that if they still hadn't found them in an hour, they should call me here.'

At that very moment, a young police trainee knocked on the door of the room.

'Come in!' Frutos called out.

The girl was glancing around, looking for Inspector Navarro.

'Sir, the security company called asking for you. I told them you were in a meeting. They told me they haven't been able to get hold of them. They said you would understand.'

'Thank you very much. I do understand.'

And the girl closed the door and walked away.

'Was it them and they scarpered with the loot?' Frutos asked.

'We need a warrant so we can send a patrol car to the homes of these two,' said Navarro.

'I'll take care of the formalities.'

It occurred to Navarro that they could speed up the process.

'Sir, while you take care of the paperwork, is it all right if I go ahead and visit the address? I imagine that by the time I get there, we'll have the warrant, won't we?'

'Yes, that's a good idea,' replied the superintendent, a little irritated. It was the second time that day that the inspector had told him what to do. 'What else?'

'For the moment, we have to check the fingerprints, cross-reference them, and if some turn up that shouldn't be there, we'll have something. We'll also take a closer look at the personal lives of the domestic staff. The fact that they entered with a key suggests there was an accomplice on the inside. For the moment, we don't have much more, sir.'

'All right, Navarro. If there are any new developments, let me know, OK?'

'Of course.'

Once the meeting was over, Frutos went to his office. At the same time as he was processing the warrant to enter the homes of the two guards who were not answering their phones, he arranged for patrols to arrive, as per the warrant, at their premises. It was essential to contact them and subject them to interrogation. That's why Navarro was heading there. The robbery occurred during their shift and they must have had something to do with it.

An hour later he received a call from Inspector Navarro:

'Superintendent, about those two security guards...'

'Yes, what is it?'

'They've been murdered.'

'Both of them?!'

'Yes, sir.'

'Right. Thanks.'

9. The bodies are discovered

On hearing the news of the two killings, Frutos ordered Inspector Navarro to return to the police station as soon as possible. He would continue in charge of the robbery, but now that there were two murders, they would be handled by Inspector Fermín Encinas.

At the end of the conversation, he dialled the homicide extension.

'Encinas, can you come to my office, please?'

Fermín Encinas was another young inspector, attached to homicide. He was one of the new officers who had been "suggested" by his bosses to join their team. They had only been working together for a short time, but he seemed like a smart, hard-working young man. He hadn't had time to solve any particularly difficult cases yet, but it would come. He would be responsible for investigating these two new crimes.

After receiving permission from the superintendent, he entered the office and closed the door behind him.

'Let me bring you up to date, Encinas. Last night there was a burglary in a villa here in Marbella. In one of those private estates for people who are set up for life.'

'I see, sir.'

'I've just been informed that the two security guards who were scheduled to be on duty there last night have been found murdered at their homes.'

'Good God!' was the reaction from Encinas on hearing about the killings.

'Inspector Navarro is going to lead the investigation into the burglary. I want you to be in charge of the murders.'

'Very good, sir.'

'Do you know each other?'

'Yes, sir. Eduardo and I often play golf together,' admitted Encinas.

It didn't take Navarro long to return to the police station, as Frutos had instructed. He went straight to the chief's office. There he discovered his colleague Fermín.

'Superintendent. Hi Fermín.'

'Please take a seat.'

Frutos put forward the hypothesis that seemed most logical: it was a robbery with the murder of the presumed thieves to eliminate any loose ends. The dead bodies were the thieves and there had been a settling of scores? Something didn't go according to plan? It was still too soon, even for hypotheses. They had to wait for the reports and the autopsies. After these remarks, he continued:

'The burglary is being investigated by Navarro and you, Encinas, will be in charge of the murders.'

'Great!'

'That's best, because the two of you will be working together. Each one in his own area but sharing information. These two events are related to each other.'

'That's excellent, sir. No problem.'

'Encinas, I need you to go to both crime scenes as soon as possible and gather as much information as you can. Once you have that information, let me know, OK?'

'Yes, of course'.

'Thank you. You may go, Encinas.'

'Navarro, did we get anything from the security cameras at the residential complex?'

'We have something, but I don't think it's much use.'

'Tell me more.'

'The video shows two security guards entering and leaving the house where the incident took place. But you can't see their faces clearly. It was at night, they were in shadow and, besides, they were doing a lot to avoid being on camera.'

'How did the guards get into the house?'

'With a key. Apparently, some homeowners provide a key to their houses. They are usually people who either don't live there all year round or travel a lot.'

'That's yet another key and now we have two dead guards,' Frutos pointed out. 'Were they in uniform?'

'Yes, they were.'

'What time are these images from?'

'Around three in the morning. From there they went to the checkpoint to finish their shift and left.'

'So they were killed afterwards.'

'That's what it looks like, sir.'

'Have you checked the identity of the guards?'

'Yes. Everything seems to be in order.'

'OK. On the subject of the key, do we know who among the household staff has keys to the entrance?'

'Only the butler, sir. After the owner, he has the most authority in that house'.

'Do you suspect him?'

'Not at the moment. We've checked his past and he's clean. Not even a traffic fine. He has no vices and if he had, he could afford to pay for them with his salary. He has been employed in various homes, always by wealthy people, and he has always had excellent references. In his type of work, that's fundamental.'

Frutos pondered for a few moments, until he finally suggested:

'Could it be possible that someone made a copy of the key without him realising?'

'Perhaps, sir. Although it would be very risky. They would have to remove the key, which I imagine the butler always carries with him, make a copy and then return it to its original place. And all without him noticing.'

'Does the key have any special features? Anything that could identify it?'

'What have you got in mind, Superintendent?'

'Let's imagine that the accomplice was indeed able to do all that and make a copy. Maybe if we investigate among the local businesses, we can find out something useful.'

'When we were in the house, I remember that the forensic team made a copy of the key. They were the ones, remember, who stated categorically that the door had been opened with the key. That's why they took photos. We can examine it and see if any of the local key cutters have seen one like that. But theoretically there's another possibility.'

'What's that, Navarro.'

'Drug the butler. Put him to sleep and put him out of action for as long as necessary.'

'That's possible too. I've already considered that, but we can't prove it. We don't know when it happened, if it did, and so there would be no trace of it left.'

'Yes, you're right. Besides, you'd have to prove who did it, and that, even with some fingerprints, would be difficult to present before a court of law. I think our best bet is to follow up on the shop lead right now. Let's just hope we get lucky.'

'The security guards' key is a weak link in the system,' said Navarro. 'We need to dig into that too. And there's one more thing.'

'Go on.'

'The footage from the security checkpoint shows the two guards getting into a car and driving away. I don't know if it's important, but in order not to leave any loose ends, we're checking the number plate.'

'Good. We'll have to wait for the autopsy. Maybe it will give us something we don't yet know. Tomorrow's another day, Navarro. Thank you very much. Get a good night's rest.'

'Thanks, sir. You too.'

When he was alone again, he turned to his laptop. The personal one, not the office one. And began to type.

Two bodies discovered. Suspected accomplice inside the house. Only one specific picture stolen. Inspector Eduardo Navarro investigating the robbery. Inspector Fermín Encinas, the murders.

10.   Daniel visits the prison

Among the countless friends, acquaintances and diverse contacts that Daniel Olavarría cultivated was a "colleague" - if you could call him that - by the name of Stefano di Bari, who he visited periodically in Alhaurín prison. Convicted of theft and trafficking in works of art, inmate number 29648 was a well-known art thief who had "worked" all over Europe. He had been sentenced to four years after being set up and having fallen into the trap like he was born yesterday. Although the benefits he enjoyed in prison included a swimming pool, sports facilities, television in the cell and a special menu, he preferred to collaborate with the police and the Guardia Civil in exchange for a shorter stay in this excellent hotel.

Daniel used to visit him once a month. He felt a little sorry for him, although he always looked remarkably well, but he kept up the contact because despite being locked away he was an almost inexhaustible source of rumours and, on occasions, of reliable advance information. He used to bring him tobacco, to ease his stay and, of course, so that he could carry out transactions in that unique market that was part of everyday life at Alhaurín prison.

The block in which Stefano was held was what the rest of the prisoners called the VIP section. Bankers, politicians, artists, businessmen, financial experts and others made up this strange mix of people with few or no scruples.

According to prison rules, all packages destined for prisoners had to pass through the scanner. Daniel, in addition to tobacco for his friend

Stefano, always left a bag for the guards containing a good bottle of expensive wine, whisky or champagne. He said it was to thank them for their kindness and they were delighted to accept it.

The meeting between them took place in one of the booths set up for the purpose. A place where, in spite of everything, they could keep what they talked about strictly confidential.

They only had twenty minutes so Daniel cut straight to the chase and asked him if he had heard anything about the robbery. Stefano looked this way and that, to make sure no one else could overhear the conversation and then answered in a low voice:

'There's a real buzz around here. Some say it was the Russians.'

'The Russian mafia? And since when did the mafia start stealing works of art? Is it for a collector?'

'I didn't say anything about the mafia,' said Stefano raising his eyebrows.

Daniel was taken aback by the reply and was left waiting for an explanation or some further detail. Stefano came to his aid.

'It's just rumours, but they say there are some very important people linked to this. Who has more power than the Russian mafia?' Stefano asked.

The question brought a look of shock and disbelief to Daniel's face.

'You mean...'

'Yes, that's who I'm talking about. What no one can explain is the motive.'

'Anyone know what's happened to the picture that was stolen?'

'It's almost certainly already left Spain. In fact, there are bets to see who can guess how long it took to get it out of the country. I said thirty minutes.'

'Thirty?'

'Or even less.'

'By car to Gibraltar?'

'By yacht.'

Daniel's face expressed increasing surprise. He didn't know if the information was correct, but it would do no harm to follow it up.

'Any rumours about the buyer?'

'No idea. But that picture is worth fifty million euros or more. That's gives us a bit of a clue.'

'And the people behind it, is that information kosher?'

'Well, their involvement is always kept strictly off the record, but there is one very significant fact.'

'Tell me.'

'The Mafia guys in here, they're scared to death. Apparently, the security guards have a lot of friends within the organisation. And who's a Russian mafioso afraid of? That's right.'

'I get it. I need to check on the guards and their connection to the mafia, even if it's indirect. And this idea of a yacht. I'll talk to Frutos. You OK with that?'

'Yeah, I reckon so.'

'Do you want to stay out of the picture or do I say something to him to see if they'll reduce your sentence?'

'At the moment, don't say anything concrete to him. If it goes well, then yes.'

'OK, that's a deal. You can count on me.'

The strident blast of a horn signalled that their time was up.

11.   Grigori and Vasili scarper

As dawn began to break, Vasili and Grigori took the opportunity to fill up with petrol and have breakfast at one of the few service stations that were open at that time of day. It was Vasili who drove there and the fact is that neither of them were quite sure where they were. Worse still, they hadn't decided where to go either. The only thing that mattered to them was that they had managed to get out of there alive.

The cafeteria at that hour was frequented only by lorry drivers and there weren't many of them. They ordered the number one breakfast combo from the menu: two fried eggs, pork escalope and fried potatoes, accompanied by coffee. They didn't want any alcohol to avoid any trouble if they were pulled over for a control by the Guardia Civil.

They chose a place at the back of the room, near the toilets, somewhere out of the way and discreet. From there they could keep an eye on the people who came in and they could see the flow of cars and lorries through the window.

After satisfying his hunger and ordering a second cup of coffee, Grigori broke the silence.

'Do you know where we're headed?'

'Does it matter?'

'Not really. I just wondered. D'you have any ideas? Among other things, we'll have to find accommodation and a job. And what money we've got won't go far.'

'Well, we'll see. Between the two of us we have almost eight thousand euros. We've spent very little of the five thousand they gave us. It's not enough to live on for the rest of our lives, but loosen up, my friend, it'll be fine. Besides, what we have to do is to take one step at a time, and you're asking me about step seven. The first move was to get out of there. We got out of there and we're still alive, which I think is no mean feat. And now comes step two.'

'OK. And that is?'

'We must choose a place where no one will think to look for us. How do you fancy the beach?'

'For God's sake, Vasili! Is this really the moment to be worrying about your tan?'

'I'm planning to live a better life than I have so far. If we get a job and a roof over our heads, what could be better than being by the beach for our days off.'

'OK then. I love the beach! So, what now?'

'You're so fucking impatient, Grigori! Has anyone ever told you that? Any suggestions, or do I have to come up with everything?'

For a moment or two there was silence. Vasili was convinced that his friend wasn't going to come up with a better option. And an idea came into his head, but since they had dumped their mobiles, they would have to resort to old-fashioned methods rather than Google Maps.

'Do we have a road atlas in the car?'

'Of course we do.'

'Do me a favour and go and fetch it. At least make some effort to help, can't you?'

Grigori reluctantly went to the car and took the atlas from the glove compartment. As he went back inside, he saw a Guardia Civil patrol car arriving on the scene. His legs began to shake.

He made his way to the table where Vasili was waiting, trying not to run. Before sitting down, he pointed out the presence of the traffic police with a quick movement of his head. Vasili gestured with his hands to tell him to stay calm. There was nothing to worry about. But certainly, this was not the time to open the map to decide where they were going to live. There was a risk that, given their obvious Russian appearance, the officers would see the road atlas open on the table and come over to help them out. They just had to wait a little longer until they had to go back to work and drove off in their patrol car again. Grigori put the atlas next to him on the couch, hiding it from sight. The officers made a visual sweep of the room and when one of them stared at him, Vasili, who was looking straight at them, nodded his head in greeting. A gesture that was reciprocated. Grigori then got up and went to the toilet, which was at the end of the bar, very close by. Vasili was pretty sure the officers had assumed they were the drivers of one of the lorries outside, several of which had foreign number plates. After a cup of coffee, the traffic police said goodbye to the waiter and continued on their patrol. At that moment Grigori return from the toilet.

'Feel better for that?' Vasili asked him mockingly.

'My stomach must be a bit upset.'

'Yes, fine. Spare me the details. Come on, give me the map, Iceman.'

Vasili looked for the relevant section of the atlas and began to search. After a few minutes of flipping pages back and forth, he made a decision.

'Rota'

'Who's a rotter?' Grigori asked confused.

'No, Rota. It's a village. A small one. That's where the American naval base is. Doesn't it ring a bell?'

'Oh yes, it does now. And why there?'

'It has a beach.'

'Awesome. Is it the only place with a beach?'

'No, but it looks like it's the sort of place we could get work, too. There are golf courses and an industrial estate. That's potential employment. We could go and take a look and then see what we decide.'

Grigori wasn't convinced by his friend's arguments, but at the end of the day, it didn't make any difference one way or the other. Just as long as no one bothered them.

12.   The police gather leads

Encinas spent most of the day investigating the two murders at the crime scenes. Fortunately, the houses were not far from each other, but it still took him the rest of the day. The next day, he returned to the police station to report to Frutos and update his colleague Navarro. As soon as he entered, the officer at the reception desk handed him an envelope.

'Inspector, this has been left for you,' he said as he held out his hand with the letter.

Encinas saw that it was indeed addressed to him: *Fermín Encinas, Inspector.*

'Who brought it?'

'A messenger delivered it. We x-rayed it and it looks clean.'

'Do we know the sender?'

'No. Sorry.'

'OK. Thanks,' and he put the mysterious envelope in the inside pocket of his jacket. He would open it later.

At the start of the follow-up meeting with Frutos and Navarro, Encinas gave them the background information.

'Both guards were shot in the head and killed. None of the local residents heard anything. No screams or the sounds of any fighting. They were neighbours who were never any trouble. The access doors had not been forced, which indicated that they knew the killer or killers. If no one heard gunshots, presumably they were fired with a silencer. There was no sign of a struggle inside, nor was there any sign that they had been trying to cover something up. The objective was to eliminate them.'

'Do we know their names?' Frutos asked.

'Vladimir Kozlov and Sergei Markovic.'

'Russians?' Frutos asked.

'Yes, and apparently with mafia connections.'

'Do the security companies take on people like that?'

'Apparently they carry out an exhaustive study before hiring them. Besides, it seems that there are more criminals inside these luxury estates than outside of them,' said Encinas.

'You're probably right about that. Do we have a time of death?' Frutos inquired.

'Forensics say around 20:00 or 20:30.'

'Are you sure?'

'That's what they say.'

'If that's true, we have yet another problem,' said Frutos.

'They were not the thieves. The security footage shows the two guards at three o'clock in the morning, seven hours after they were killed,' Encinas pointed out.

'That suggests that these two guards were impersonated by the real thieves, the ones in the video.'

'But what about the security company? Didn't they notice? Surely they have to show their ID cards and have to sign the log sheet?' Navarro asked.

'What if the ID was a convincing fake? With the correct format and the right name, but the photo changed. After all, who really takes these controls seriously? Once they become an everyday routine, irregularities of this kind occur. The only reliable system would be for whoever carries out the control to know the real guards personally so that they notice the substitution,' argued Encinas.

'We are going to have to look more closely at the guys from the security company. Something is fishy here.'

'Yes,' continued Navarro. 'We've also learned another important piece of information.'

'Go on.'

'You remember I mentioned the car the security guards were using? We ran the plates and it turns out it was stolen the day before the robbery. I've already given orders for all patrols to look out for it.'

'Let's hope we get lucky and they didn't torch it. We might get some prints. Do we know anything more about the key belonging to the butler?' the superintendent prompted.

'Not yet sir, I've got several officers checking any shops that cut keys, covering the area from Marbella to San Pedro. It will take a while before we know the results.'

Frutos was a meticulous man. He was rigorous in his approach, but even so, his inspectors were aware that the investigation was not moving along as fast as it should. Twenty-four hours had passed and they already had two dead bodies, a stolen picture, a stolen car that was still missing and they had not yet identified the actual thieves. In fact, they didn't even know if the thieves were still alive. They were bogged down.

'It would appear that we can't do much more than wait for events to unfold,' said the superintendent.

The remark stunned the young detectives. This was not the attitude that was expected of a superintendent in charge of a dual investigation into a robbery and a double murder. It was Encinas who, after a couple of minutes thinking in silence, said:

'If someone steals something, it's reasonable to suppose that they get paid for it, right?'

It was a rhetorical question that did not require an answer. And he continued with his deductive reasoning.

'We know that the painting is worth a great deal, and as far as we can tell, the job has been organized by experts and ruthless criminals. So, there is no shortage of money available. In that case, the thieves must have been well paid, right?'

'I see where you're going, Encinas,' said the superintendent. 'You want us to follow the trail of the money.'

'Exactly. At the moment we don't know if they are dead or alive, but it is reasonable to assume that at some point they will have received the contract money and spent it.'

'I'll put more officers on it and ask for collaboration from the local police to see who has been spending more money than usual,' said Frutos. And he continued: 'It's not that I don't have confidence in you, but if you show up in your uniforms and cars asking questions, I don't think you're going to be very successful.'

'OK. We'll set it up differently and visit bars, nightclubs, strip clubs, etc.'

'Good, let's start there and see what happens.'

Once again both police officers were taken aback by what they were beginning to perceive as a lack of professionalism. There were other avenues that could be part of the investigation that had not been pursued.

They looked at each other as if they had already discussed their views beforehand. Finally Navarro made a suggestion:

'Sir, if it's all right with you, I've just had an idea. We could leak some details to the media, both the press and the TV. Shake the tree and see what falls out. We'll present the robbery and the murder as one event, not two. And if we show the images of the guards and the car they used, we might elicit some response.'

'If they see themselves on TV, they're bound to get nervous,' said Encinas.

'Assuming they're still alive,' said Frutos. 'That's fine with me. Go ahead with that.'

Once they'd left the office, Frutos logged back on to his personal computer:

There are plenty of leads. Things are getting more complicated. We continue to investigate.

As they were leaving, Navarro asked his colleague:

'Fancy a coffee?'

'Yes, but not in here. Let's go outside.'

'As they left the police station, they instinctively headed for the coffee shop they and their colleagues regularly used.'

'No. Let's go to another one. There are too many people here,' Encinas told his companion.

'Strictly confidential?'

'Yes.'

They took a short walk to a café behind the police station where they were less likely to see their colleagues and sat down on the terrace. Noticing the time, they decided to take the opportunity to grab a bite to eat while they were there.

'What do you think about what happened in there?' Encinas asked his golfing buddy.

'What do you mean?'

'Didn't you get the feeling that the superintendent was content just to sit back and let things happen?'

'Well, actually, I had a similar feeling yesterday, in the residential complex. I got the impression that he wanted to go back to his office without talking to the security guards. I think he's thinking more about his retirement. You don't get to a position like that by just letting things happen. What are you worried about?'

'What worries me is this casual attitude. We've got a robbery and a double murder and we've got nothing. And he's so unconcerned about it.'

'Come on mate, we've only just started. Aren't you being a bit demanding?'

'Well, look at this, for example. We have the names of two Russians, murdered in their own home, with a bullet in the head. They are two security guards, not only are they foreign but they're connected to the mafia and now they're dead. Don't you think it would be more normal to contact Interpol immediately?'

Navarro sat staring at him for a few moments. Just as he was about to answer, the waiter arrived with the first course, a seafood cocktail. He waited for him to move away from the table.

'OK, yes, maybe you're right. But perhaps he's already done that and just hasn't told us yet.'

'So who's running this investigation, me, him, both of us or no-one?'

Navarro was beginning to understand his colleague's point of view. He said nothing, which was as good as a agreeing with everything he had said.

'What are you going to do?' Navarro asked.

'My job. ALL of my job.'

'And what does that mean, tough guy?'

'You'll find out in due time, my friend. Now let's eat and stop talking about work. This is better than I expected,' he said, referring to the cocktail.

'How about a round of golf this weekend?'

'You're on'.

The investigation had barely started and most of it was on hold. They had to wait for the ballistics people to tell them about the bullets found in the bodies. They had to wait to see if the car turned up anything, prints, DNA, anything at all. They had to follow the trail of the money they assumed had been paid. It was a frustrating feeling to have so many fronts open and to be waiting for information, waiting to get some form of result.

'How about we go out this afternoon and knock a few balls about?' asked Fermín.

'Do you feel the need to hit something?'

'Yes, I do. These things really mess my head up. Sometimes I feel like I want to move things along faster than I should. It really stresses me out.'

'Well, it's not a very good state of mind to play golf in. You'll probably leave the club feeling worse than when you went in.'

'It's my way of calming down, I concentrate on the game and it helps me relax. Other people like to do yoga or transcendental meditation.'

'OK, you've convinced me. While we're at it, we could ask if anyone's heard anything. Mind you, I doubt that the killer is the type that spends time playing golf, but you never know.'

'If you think that's going to give us an excuse for bunking off from the police station all afternoon, I think you're mistaken, mate. I don't think Frutos is going to buy it.'

'The truth is there's bugger all else we can do right now.'

'You're right about that.'

Hours later, after hitting a few balls at the golf club, Fermín Encinas' composure began to return, albeit slowly. Concentrating on his shots on the driving range helped to distract his thoughts from the investigation for a while. As this happened, his accuracy increased, which, in turn, produced a further positive effect on his mood. After the practice session, being as much friends as colleagues, they decided to go for a drink in Puerto Banús. And while they were at it, like a pair of insurance salesmen knocking on doors, they discreetly asked their contacts if they had seen or heard anything out of the ordinary in the last few days.

Once he was back at home Encinas went through the unconscious routine that he had developed over time. He took out his regulation weapon, a 9mm USP compact, removed the magazine, extracted the round from the chamber and then replaced the magazine. Finally he put the whole thing away in a drawer in the living room bookcase.

Walking through to the bedroom, he took off his jacket and it was then that he saw the envelope he had been given in the morning at the police station. He had forgotten about it, but now it intrigued him. It was a letter hand-delivered by a courier, with no stamp and no return address.

When he opened it, his surprise and scepticism increased.

Inside, there was a folded sheet of paper and when he unfolded it, he found something resembling a typewritten hieroglyphic.

"USER ID: Tatiana_Kovalenko@gmail.com

PASSWORD: babushka"

That's all he needed! As if it wasn't bad enough that the girls from the night clubs left flyers in the car or in his letterbox at home, now they had gone one step further and left a letter addressed to him personally at the police station.

But then, while his gaze was still fixed on the sheet of paper as if it had mesmerized him, he began to reflect: who would go to the trouble of writing this, putting it in an envelope, putting my name and position on it, hiring a courier and having it delivered to me at the police station, instead of sending it by post?

Even at the risk of it being a typical SPAM that might damage his PC, he let his curiosity get the better of him. He had total confidence in his antivirus. Besides, at the police station, they had added a few more tools to ensure confidentiality. So, he sat down in front of his computer, and went to Gmail. He typed in the username and password.

In the inbox was just the typical welcome message. Nothing else. But he looked at the Draft folder. It was showing one item.

He clicked on it and saw a message waiting to be sent. When he opened it, he couldn't believe what he was reading.

13.   The *IRINA* arrives in Monaco

After a couple of days of sailing, exactly as anticipated the yacht *Irina* arrived from Marbella at Port Hercules, Monaco's pleasure harbour, with her precious cargo securely locked away.

As soon as the docking manoeuvre was completed and the engines stopped, Yuri set foot ashore and looked for a public telephone. He called the number of Ivan Orlov, his boss. When he answered, he uttered the phrase they had agreed on: "your friend is now here". Ivan's reply was an address, which his right-hand man memorized. He then returned aboard, went to his cabin, opened the safe, took out the package that had been delivered to him in Marbella, which he had not unpacked, and put it in a briefcase with a chain attached to his wrist. In Monaco, such sights were commonplace. It would not attract attention.

Before going ashore again, he instructed the crew to take two or three days off. Then he headed for a taxi rank. As he got into the vehicle, he gave the address Ivan had provided on the phone.

The destination was a three-storey, modern-style villa on the edge of the cliffs, bordered by a row of tall, leafy trees at the back of the house and the ocean at the front. The main entrance was equipped with a bulletproof sentry box from which the identity of anyone wishing to enter was monitored. The guard approached the taxi and Yuri pronounced the code word: *Irina*.

The security guard returned to his sentry box and when he received authorization, the gates opened up. The taxi driver continued to the top of the drive, apparently not especially impressed by the surroundings. He must have been accustomed to visiting villas like this, with splendid, lavishly manicured gardens and statues and sculptures of dubious quality, scattered among the lush greenery. Yuri paid the fare, giving him an excellent tip, and the taxi driver left the property by the same entrance.

As soon as he stepped through the threshold of the front door of the house, two heavies practically leapt on him and frisked him. They also asked him to open his briefcase. When he opened it, the bodyguard wanted him to unpack the object to check that there was nothing dangerous hidden in it. Yuri shook his head with a firm "no" as he closed the briefcase. The gorilla then bent his right arm at the elbow and spoke to his wrist. He spoke in French and after a few seconds, after receiving instructions, he allowed Yuri to continue on his way.

After walking a few steps, he came across another massive door made of solid, carved wood. When it opened, he could see a large living room and in the background a terrace and the Mediterranean Sea. He made his way down the three steps that separated him from his boss and the owner of the villa. He greeted them both and, opening the handcuff on his wrist, handed the briefcase to Ivan Orlov. The latter thanked him for his work and told him that he could go to the kitchen and have something to eat, in the company of the rest of the bodyguards who were protecting the proprietor of the house.

Mahfuz Amirmoez, the owner of the villa, was a Qatari multimillionaire and a compulsive purchaser of works of art, even though he didn't really understand anything about art. For him, the most important thing was the outlay he had had to make in order to show off in front of his friends and acquaintances. He was not interested in any particular style, nor in building up a collection that made any artistic sense. He was only interested in filling the innumerable gaps on the walls around his palace in Doha, the capital. It was a monster of a palace with 130 bedrooms, all with their own en suite bathrooms, with gleaming displays of gold throughout, marble floors, a helipad, two swimming pools, one saltwater and one freshwater, and a nine-hole golf course on his estate.

He travelled in his private jet or, depending on where he was going to spend his leisure time, he would give directions to the captain of his yacht to take him, so that he could also enjoy long cruises at sea.

The size and extravagances of the yacht were commensurate with the palace in which he lived. The boat was 105 metres long and 30 metres wide and among other eccentricities it had a swimming pool, a Jacuzzi, a room rigged out as a cinema and another solely used to stage shows.

Mahfuz was in contact with all the dealers who had any works of art to sell, irrespective of whether they were the legal or not so legal owners of the piece in question. These characters, meanwhile, hovered like birds of prey around him, offering him - in most cases - crude copies of masterpieces, which the millionaire paid for at the price of the original, to the delight of the sellers and the greater pride of the buyer, who had one more painting to show off to his guests at the next party.

 Thus, in this simple manner, as soon as the rumour reached him that a work attributed to a certain Dürer was for sale for sixty million euros, he showed his interest in acquiring it. For the Russian secret service, finding a buyer profile such as this was a no-brainer, it was simply a gift from heaven.

Once Ivan Orlov had taken the briefcase that Yuri had given him, he removed the painting from it, still wrapped up and protected as per the instructions that the thieves had received. The only thing that mattered to Yuri was that this man with a dark complexion, black eyes, thinning hair and prominent belly, parted with the agreed sum. He didn't care about anything else. Meanwhile, the buyer, who was not very clear about who Dürer was, was only interested in hanging it in his palace and broadcasting to the world what it had cost him.

In any case, and just for the sake of form, they had agreed that a couple of experts from each side would examine the work and certify its authenticity. The Russians did not want any trouble from someone who claimed to be related to the Qatari royal family.

The two gentlemen descended the stairs to the floor below. On the way down, two individuals who looked like university professors joined them and they all entered a room that was lit only by a skylight high up on the wall. It was an entirely bug-proof room and the walls were lined with aluminium foil. Next, the academic-looking individuals donned white gloves and with a magnifying glass pressed to their eye, began to examine the drawing, the paper, the characteristics, the date. They used a microscope, some sort of powder, consulted some books they had with them and after an hour, both came to an agreement: it was authentic. The artwork was by Dürer.

Mahfuz Amirmoez was ready to make a transfer to a bank account in the Cayman Islands for the amount of sixty million euros and that made him immensely happy because it made him the new owner of this masterpiece. He didn't care if it was stolen or not.

As soon as Ivan had confirmation that the money had been received, he issued a document acknowledging the transaction. That would be the only proof that such an event had taken place. As a matter of protocol, all that remained was for him to inform his superiors of the operation. And that was what he was going to do. In person. In Moscow.

14.   Daniel and Frutos

Between the doubts he had begun with and the time he had spent sorting out his ideas to draw up a draft plan, almost a week had passed since the robbery. During those days he also heard about the murders, and that had already started to worry him. He had an appointment coming up with Bukowski. But first, he had to see his friend Superintendent Frutos to pass on certain information and get an update on his progress.

The prison visit to his friend and former colleague in crime, Stefano di Bari, had provided Daniel with a jumping-off point for his investigation. It wasn't even a solid basis to begin from, it seemed more like a rumour, one of the many that circulate in the corridors of prisons, but at least he had somewhere to start. Besides, his friend knew perfectly well how to identify a false rumour, one of those hoaxes that are spread to detect who has a loose tongue. He was quite capable of differentiating that from the real thing and that gave Daniel a certain degree of reassurance.

Inside the prison it was rumoured that Russians had been the perpetrators of the robbery. Stefano also informed him of the gossip about the murders of the security guards, information that, in principle, did not interest Daniel. His friend Stefano had however given him a piece of information that he had to check: that the stolen drawing had been taken out on a private yacht. This was, in his opinion, the quickest and most efficient way to do it. If it had happened at night and they hadn't noticed the theft and the murders until the next morning, the sketch was already a long way off.

What had left him more concerned was his friend's insistence that the perpetrators were more dangerous than the Russian mafia itself. At this point, he thought it appropriate to have a chat with his friend Frutos, the chief superintendent of the Marbella police.

The two had known each other for many years. Through their respective professional obligations they had had the opportunity to work together on several occasions, and this had resulted in a healthy friendship based on mutual respect. Moreover, they needed each other.

'Hello, Superintendent, how are you?' said Daniel when Frutos picked up the phone. 'Thank you for taking my call, I know you're a busy man.'

'I'm fine, thank you. Nice to hear your voice after so long. In fact, I was being to worry that you hadn't rung before now.'

'Haha. As always! Well, the truth is, you're right. I could really use a chat with you and, besides, I think I have something that might be useful to you.'

'That sounds good to me. Let's have lunch together sometime.'

'I'd like that, but let's set a date and time now.'

'Tomorrow at 2.30, is that OK with you?'

'Yes, that's great, thanks. Whose turn is it to pay?' Daniel asked.

'It's your turn.'

'Are you sure about that?'

'No, but I've just decided, to avoid any arguments.'

'Haha. OK. Same place as usual?'

'Yes. I don't want to be seen eating in a public place with someone from the private sector. There's always someone who wants to cause trouble.'

'Understood. I'll see you there.'

For situations like this, there was a restaurant Frutos preferred to use where the owner had also been a policeman. It was some distance from the police station, which gave him a certain degree of privacy, and they always had a table reserved for him in a secluded area, to avoid prying eyes and possible gossip. That was the place he used for such encounters and that was where he had arranged to meet Daniel.

Daniel arrived first and after greeting the head waiter and the owner, both of whom he knew well, he sat down to wait for his friend. Since the place was known for its excellent fish and seafood, he ordered a good white wine in advance to save time. Frutos arrived promptly and after the customary greetings, they toasted the success of their work, placed their orders and began to catch up with each other's news.

When they were almost at dessert Daniel brought up the real subject of the meeting. He wanted to tell the superintendent about the information he had obtained and see if his friend could also contribute something that might help him in the search for the stolen picture. As soon as Daniel mentioned the Russians, he noticed, almost imperceptibly, how Frutos hid a gesture of concern. There was information he couldn't share with Daniel because it was an ongoing investigation.

For example, the 9 mm bullets extracted from the bodies of the murdered guards were known to belong to a unique Makarov pistol, of Russian manufacture. They didn't know the owner, but it had already been involved in other incidents on the Costa del Sol, namely the murder of a mafia individual, in a case that had been closed unsolved due to lack of evidence. Nor could he share with Daniel that the car they had used to escape had been stolen the day before and that, inside it, they had found a real gold mine: the uniforms they used, the false ID cards and even the maps that helped them to get to the residential estate, to identify the villa and to know where the picture was hanging.

After a lot of research and pounding the streets, they had also learned that the person who had ordered a copy of the key to be made, so that the burglars could enter through the front door, was a woman. All this suggested an accomplice acting from inside the house. A current member of staff or a disgruntled ex-employee with a desire for revenge or acting on the promise of a good reward.

And the officers had also confirmed that two individuals, who looked Eastern European, had been seen hanging around in nightclubs they did not usually frequent and spending a lot of money. Encinas interpreted this to mean that these could be the perpetrators of the robbery and perhaps the double murder, who having been paid for their work were celebrating in style.

He had instructed his inspectors to leak some details of the events to the press and TV. He hoped that the cooperation of the public would yield results and at the same time, if those who had fled felt they were being pursued, that they would be caught making a mistake.

With all that and what Daniel had just told him, it was clear that this was about Russians. Either bad or very bad, but Russians.

'There's one thing I would suggest, Daniel. I think it's best that you stick to chasing down the stolen picture and identifying the thieves. We'll be in constant contact and you can keep me up to date. And I'll focus on the investigation of the murders, which is quite enough to keep me busy for the moment.'

'That's fine with me. I'll see how far I can get, because if what I've been told...'

'Who told you about the Russians, Daniel?'

'A friend of mine.'

'Okay. Go on, then.'

'...if what I've been told is true, we'll see what happens when I meet them. I hope they don't decide to remove me from the picture.'

'I hope not. I'm sure they won't. Right, we'll do that, then?'

'Agreed. First thing I'm going to do is go back and talk to the victim of the robbery. After that, I'll get stuck into the chase.'

'OK. Be careful, Daniel.'

'I will.'

Returning to his office late in the afternoon, Frutos sat down at his personal computer.

Yacht IRINA targeted in enquiry. Russians suspected.

15.   Vasili and Grigori in Rota

After a long night full of anxiety and fear, followed by a morning that was just as fraught, the two friends managed to get away from Marbella unscathed and arrive in a town where no one would look for them.

The first thing they did was find a mobile phone shop to buy two prepaid Sims. They had thrown theirs away when they left the getaway car.

Straight away, they started looking for accommodation, using their mobile phones, which, thanks to Google, was fast and easy. They reckoned that being foreigners, if they tried to rent a flat without a work contract, they would get nowhere. So they searched the internet and found a guesthouse that was not too expensive. While they were looking for a job, at least they had a place to sleep. When they arrived at the place they were delighted to find that it was almost right on the beach.

'Look Grigori. Just what we were looking for. A place by the beach,' said Vasili, smiling broadly and looking chuffed to bits.

His friend looked at him and shook his head as if to say "this guy is getting more insane every day. With everything we've got to worry about and all he can think of is the beach."

After settling into the guesthouse they decided it was time for lunch. When they had arrived in the town they had seen a huge burger restaurant and so they went there. It was virtually empty. They ordered a couple of burgers each with all the extras and two large beers and sat down in front of a TV that had the volume turned down. It was going to be a nice meal. They were seated in such a way that Vasili was facing the TV and Grigori had his back to it. At one point Vasili almost choked when he saw a news item on the TV and read the subtitles: "Robbery in a Marbella villa". This was followed by images of two men, dressed in security uniforms, getting into a car with the number plate clearly visible. And to round off the meal, the news programme said, according to the subtitles, that two security guards had been murdered in their homes and that it was believed that the men in the pictures were the thieves and killers. It was at that point that Vasili stopped eating.

'What's the matter, mate? Weren't you that hungry?'

'Yes, but I'm stuffed now.'

The truth is that Vasili had totally lost his appetite.

'But you've only eaten one burger and you haven't even touched the other one.'

'I'll ask for it to be wrapped up and take it back for dinner.'

'Are you all right, Vasili? You look pale.'

'No. I'm fine. It's just that I ate too fast. It probably didn't do me any good.'

Vasili didn't want to say anything to his friend because he knew him and he knew he would lose his nerve. When he was freaked out he was capable of the most stupid things you could imagine. One of them being worried was enough. But they had a problem, that was clear. That guy, bloody Oleg, didn't tell them that two guards were going to be killed and now, all of a sudden, they were wanted for a crime they hadn't committed. It was one thing to steal and another to shoot and kill people. Had it been a tip-off? From whom? From this Oleg? Why? Did he want to throw them to the police dogs and thus get them out of the way and keep himself in the clear?

'Man, what's wrong with you? You're staring at the TV with a face like a zombie and you've left your food. You look like you've seen a ghost, for fuck's sake.'

He preferred not to answer.

'I'm going to the loo. I'll be right back. I think something's upset me.'

Vasili got up, went to the toilet and threw up the entire contents of his stomach. Then he returned to the table but decided that he definitely couldn't tell Grigori.

'We have to look for work, Grigori. Have you finished yet?'

'Yes. Where do we start?'

'As always, on the internet.'

Neither of them was afraid of hard work and they were willing to take on anything. So, in a town that, as Vasili had said, had plenty of job opportunities, they soon found work in a construction and renovation company, with a work contract and a salary that wasn't bad. Once they had that, they could look for a flat to rent.

As for the news item, Vasili still kept his mouth shut. And what was worse, he couldn't work out what he should do. He even questioned whether he should do something or just wait for things to calm down. For the moment, he decided on the latter.

16. Daniel and Bukowski

Just as he had told Aaron Bukowski when they first met, Daniel needed a few days to gather some information and get an idea of how he could approach the problem. Despite the conversations he had had with his friend Stefano in prison and with the superintendent, he didn't have much to go on, but at least he had somewhere to start. Be that as it may, the least he could do was visit the unfortunate victim of the theft and update him on progress.

During their meeting, Daniel gave Bukowski all the facts he had at his disposal. He told him it was suspected that the Russians were responsible, but that it was not the Mafia and that it was believed that the drawing had left Spain by sea, on a private yacht. He explained that this was the only thing he had to work on, and he had to proceed from there.

'The first thing I am going to do is to check which yachts were in the harbour and which left at dawn on the day of the robbery. If this rumour is correct, less than an hour must have elapsed between the theft and the departure of the picture from Spain. I'll speak to the director of the marina in Marbella.'

Bukowski remained thoughtful for a few moments. He rose slowly from his chair and began to walk around his office. He was mulling something over, it was obvious, but Daniel didn't want to interrupt. He kept silent, waiting to see what would ensue. Finally, he finished pacing up and down and returned to his chair.

'Mr Olavarría. My life, as you well know, has been, shall we say, eventful, but because of my business negotiations, I have had the pleasure of meeting people of very diverse backgrounds. I can say, without false modesty, that I know princes, kings and certain very influential people that you have never heard of. But I also, on occasion, come into contact with the most undesirable people you could imagine. And yet, I have to say that, despite that, these people are honest and reliable. True to their word.'

He was silent for a moment, as if to catch his breath, and Daniel profited from it.

'Mr Bukowski, I honestly don't know what you're getting at. I'm a little lost.'

'Ha-ha. I understand you. Sometimes my explanations get a little protracted. I'll get to the point. What I mean is that, from what you have told me, the thieves are dangerous people. They have murdered two people, they have robbed me and apparently, according to the rumours you have heard, they have enough money to move around on a private yacht, at least as far as we know. What I am offering you is protection and the financial means you will need. Without limit.'

Bukowski then opened a drawer in his desk and took out a finely carved wooden box and placed it on the desk. Opening it, he took out an envelope on which was written Daniel's first name, with no surname, and handed it to him.

Daniel opened the envelope and found an American Express Centurion Card, better known as the Amex Black Card, something that only very few people on the planet have. His name was printed on the card.

'I'm sorry, I don't understand.'

'That card is linked to a current account that I personally control. It has virtually no spending limit. Use it as much as you need to. It's for all the expenses you need, including, of course, pocket money.'

Daniel was stunned. He had not, at least not officially, told him that he would be taking the case, and yet the card had his name on it.

'But how did you know...'

'Mr Olavarría, when I hire someone, I usually know who I'm hiring. I was sure you would accept the assignment and not for the money.'

At that, Daniel felt a little uneasy.

And Bukowski carried on:

'That's only part of our agreement. There's another part that I mentioned earlier when I started to go off on a tangent. As I was saying,' Bukowski continued, 'I know people from all walks of life, and I think that in this case here, that is going to come in very handy. I'd like to hear from you as you progress with your enquiries. I will be helping you from here in my office.'

Daniel wondered if the poor old man's mind was starting to play tricks on him and he had begun to lose his grip on reality. Help him from that office? He might know a lot of people, but he doubted he would be of any use to him when he was travelling around Europe looking for a stolen piece of art and having to prise it out of the new owner's hands. A new owner who might be a violent Russian assassin as well as a thief.

'I see a certain scepticism on your face, Daniel. May I call you Daniel?'

'Yes, of course. Well, I confess I am rather perplexed and somewhat confused. I don't understand how I can take advantage of your generous offer to help me...'

'Believe me, Daniel, I can help and I shall demonstrate that to you. Trust me.'

With those words, Bukowski rose from his chair again, ending the conversation. He turned to Daniel and gave him his last instruction.

'Now you must go to the marina in Marbella and find out about the yacht. If they don't cooperate with you, you let me know, OK?'

'Yes, I will.'

And if you get the information you need, you tell me that too, OK?

'All right, Mr Bukowski.'

'And now, let the chase commence. Good luck.'

17.   The mole

When Fermín Encinas logged on to the email using the name and password sent to him anonymously, he was stunned by what he saw in front of him.

For now, it's better for everyone if I don't tell you my name. Please trust me and pay attention to what I am about to tell you.

This is not a trap and I'm not trying to extort money. I, too, am fighting for justice.

You have a mole in your garden. A very big mole.

Whenever you want to communicate with me, use this email. Don't send anything. Just write it and keep it as a draft.

Do not discuss this with anyone. Not friends and especially not people at work. You don't know if you might be revealing information to the mole.

The killer is not Russian. The thieves are.

M.

He sat staring at the screen of his laptop as if hypnotised.

Scanning the text, it was clear that this was a person very close to the investigation. He knew his name and his responsibility in the investigation. Apparently, the author had information that enabled him to distinguish between the singular of "killer" and the plural of "thieves". This only time and the investigation itself would clarify. But what struck him most was that he did not give names. He spoke of the mole, but without specifying anyone. Did he not know who it was? Or was it a deliberate decision? If so, why keep it a secret?

Fermín thought that perhaps his informant was only trying to tip him off so that he himself would work out who the mole was. If he had given the name, he might have been suspicious. If, however, he allowed him to investigate on his own and to make up his own mind, the conclusion would be beyond doubt. But what if it was a trap to divert his attention?

What he had no doubt about was that he should bring this information to the attention of his superior. At last he thought he had discovered the real reason why he had suddenly been given this strange assignment. And that fitted in with the anonymous note he had just read. That was what finally convinced him that the message could be genuine.

It was highly improbable, if not impossible, that anyone would know that he was an agent of the CNI (the Spanish National Intelligence Centre) who had infiltrated the Marbella police station, with the covert objective of exposing a mole, so the anonymous tip-off confirmed both its existence and the veracity of the informant himself.

Following the instructions, he replied:

Message received, loud and clear. Then he hit "Save as draft". He closed the session and, using a specially modified secure phone, called his superior in the CNI to inform him.

***

It was Friday, and in the station briefing room they had prepared a special breakfast, something that had turned into a regular routine, the main aim of which was to break the daily monotony and create an atmosphere of camaraderie and good vibes, with the approaching weekend as an excuse. It had to be said, thought Frutos, that Encinas and Navarro really did make a good team.

On the table next to the wall, there was a thermos of hot coffee, another of milk, a few light pastries for those who wanted to keep in shape, and for the rest, boxes of doughnuts of all kinds. A calorie bomb that Frutos couldn't afford but that Encinas and Navarro burned off by pounding the streets and playing golf. That atmosphere made Fridays special, the prelude to the weekend.

After a first cup of coffee and a doughnut, the world looked different. Most of the time, Frutos was content with the coffee, which was infinitely better than the black enema expelled by the dreadful machine installed in the police station.

'Do we have any prints from the getaway car?' Frutos asked, kicking off the weekly briefing.

'We do, but we haven't identified them,' replied Encinas. 'They're not registered in Spain. We've passed them on to Interpol, but we're still waiting.'

'Did you get DNA from the uniforms, as well?'

'Yes, and something much more interesting. A card from a nightclub in Puerto Banus, called *Irina La Dulce*.

'Do we know anything about who the owner is? Have we paid him a visit?'

'Not yet. We thought it would be better to wait until we've got something we can use to put pressure on him. We need a photo of the guys that left the fingerprints or something similar. If we show up just to ask, we'll raise the alarm and we might blow it.'

'Right. Do we have anything on the fake ID cards?'

'We've spoken to the security company and they say they make them themselves and that they appear to be identical to theirs.'

'Does that mean someone from the security company is an accomplice of the thieves?'

'That's what it looks like, Chief. It always seemed very bizarre to me that strangers could just walk into the housing estate with fake ID cards and nobody would say anything. Someone's been turned.'

'What about the maps we found?'

'I think they've been drawn up by two different people. One from the security company and one from inside the house. The one of the interior, where the location of the drawing is indicated, has to be from someone who's seen it. And then there's the issue of the key.'

'Apparently it was a woman, wasn't it?'

'Yes. We have a description, but it doesn't fit anyone on our list.'

'Someone in disguise?'

'Almost certainly. Whoever it was went to a lot of trouble to get the copy made. They went to the middle of nowhere for it, thinking to throw us off the scent, so it wouldn't be surprising if they also wore some kind of disguise.'

'So, we have nothing,' said Frutos, visibly frustrated.

'Well, sir, we are waiting for Interpol. I think that, if these individuals have operated in Spain, they have certainly done so in other countries. They don't seem like first-timers. If we can get a positive ID, with photos, we can go back to the place where we're told two Eastern European men were seen out drinking. They were spending money in nightclubs, where they weren't regulars. And then there's the nightclub in Puerto Banús...'

'*Irina,*' remarked Navarro, who, although keeping quiet, was paying attention.

'That's the one! When we get the Interpol report, we'll pay that club a visit.'

'Navarro, I have reason to believe that it's possible that the picture may have left Spain via Puerto Deportivo. Go and see which yachts were berthed on the day of the robbery and which ones set sail immediately after the time of the robbery. We know the time from security footage. By the way, do we have any more on that? Have the press release and the publicity given us anything useful?'

'We've had plenty of calls, but none worthy of serious consideration,' replied Navarro.

Frutos' expression turned sour, but Navarro cheered him up a bit.

'Except for one, sir. A very strange call that was left on the answering machine. A woman's voice, with an accent, and she just said two names.'

Navarro rummaged through his notes and found it.

'Vasili and Grigori.'

'Does that get us anywhere? It sounds like a joke.'

'It doesn't tell us anything at the moment. But there were no reports in the press that the suspects were Russian. And she's given us two Russian names.'

Frutos thought for a moment. That information was all very well. But even if it were correct, there was still the matter of identifying them. And, above all, who could have an interest in bringing these individuals, the alleged perpetrators of the robbery and murders, to the attention of the police?

'Well, it's not much, frankly,' said Frutos with annoyance. 'But we'll see. You, Navarro, keep on the trail of the yacht.' And looking at Encinas, 'you take a close look at the security company. Investigate their system and find out how it's been breached. We should also make more inquiries about the members of the household staff. Someone on the inside is up to their neck in it.

Have we examined their bank accounts?'

'Not yet, sir. Shall I take care of the court order?'

'Yes, you do that. Well gentlemen, anything else?'

'Yes sir,' said Encinas. 'Do you remember the mobile phone Sims we found in the abandoned stolen car?'

'Yes. Do we have something?'

'They were pretty damaged and they're trying to restore them. It will take time. Hopefully we'll have some luck.'

'Is that all? All right, then, See you next Friday. Have a good weekend.'

'Thank you, sir. You too.'

Frutos returned to his office with a worried look on his face. Things were not going as expected or as he would like them to. Again, he sat down at his computer keyboard.

The circle is tightening. Club Irina in the spotlight. Tip-off about Vasili and Grigori. Phones. Maps. Yacht. Interpol.

18.   Casting the net

Fermín Encinas reconnected to the email of his secret informer. After the briefing at the station, there remained a lot of loose ends to investigate and he wanted to see if his associate could help him.

Once he was logged in, he typed a very direct question:

'Is someone from the security company involved?'

He left it in the draft folder as before and poured himself a whisky while he waited for the answer. He didn't know whether it would take five minutes or five days, so every now and then he would log on and log off again. Until, on one occasion, there was something new waiting for him.

'The head of security for the night shift.'

The answer was clear, concise and to the point.

'Why hasn't he been arrested?' was Encinas' next question. And the answer came almost immediately.

'He's just a small fish. We want the whale.'

It was clear what their strategy was.

There was a mole, there was no doubt about it. But he wasn't a hundred per cent sure who it was. So, he considered putting everyone under surveillance.

To include all those involved would mean a large number of people and resources. But there was no alternative. In his list of suspects, he must include ALL of them, that is, Superintendent Frutos as well, no matter how scandalous it might seem. He contacted his CNI chief and made the proposal.

His superiors approved the measure.

Straight away they planted microphones in the Bukowski villa, to check if any of the staff were involved. It was easy for them to pose as policemen again and to use the excuse that they had to check some details. They bugged the kitchens, the fixed phones and the extension lines. As they already had the mobile numbers of all the staff, the telecom specialists were able to track the content of all conversations and messages.

To do this at the superintendent's house, they used the old trick that they needed to check the telephone installation. As the cleaning lady was alone and was Russian, when she saw these men in working clothes she had neither the nerve nor the authority to raise objections.

Encinas felt bad that his friend and colleague Navarro had to suffer the same kind of surveillance, but he didn't want to take any risks.

Just as they hacked into the mobiles of all the staff in the villa, they did the same with everyone else involved. Hidden cameras were also set up to monitor the comings and goings at Frutos' and Navarro's homes.

Within a couple of days, the surveillance operation was fully set up. It was just a matter of waiting for the fish to take the bait.

***

Ivan Orlov and his head of security, Yuri, said goodbye to their host and client after confirming that the money was already in the account. Then, they got into the official car of the Ukrainian consulate that Ivan used when he was in Monaco. In reality, this was the only link he had with the consulate because, in practice, he never showed up at the offices. All the administration was handled by his deputy, a very capable and efficient Ukrainian who scrupulously attended to his duties with enthusiasm and diligence.

They went to Ivan's private residence, a six-bedroom villa covering six hundred square metres, built at the beginning of the 20th century. It was in the Belle Époque style, with a hand carved facia rendered in pastel tones and it looked out over the bay of Monaco. The palatial building had three floors, a swimming pool, oak trees and olive groves. But it was the terrace overlooking the sea, offering unique views and stunning sunsets that made it such a privileged location. It was one of the most beautiful villas on the French Riviera, while its position made it easy to defend against intruders, prying journalists and unwanted visitors. The only access to the property was via a narrow, tarmac road which though only of single lane width was two-way. The road meandered parallel to the cliffs that separated it from the Mediterranean, making it a deadly hazard in its own right. It was so inaccessible that Ivan himself liked to joke: "It's the most secure and inaccessible place on the planet. It's impossible to get close by. Not a single public road passes through here. It doesn't even have an address, so no one can write to me. It's my paradise."

When they arrived at the main entrance, one of the servants opened the car door for them. They stepped out and the driver took the car to the garage where he would give it a once over to ensure it was sparkling clean, while Ivan and Yuri entered the palatial mansion and went up the marble staircase to the main floor. Ivan made his way to the terrace and opened wide the doors of the veranda. As far as the eye could see there was nothing but an endless expanse of blue sea.

They sat down in two wicker armchairs around a low coffee table, looking out over the ocean. Ivan was satisfied that everything had turned out as he had planned. It was time for a celebration. The men in Moscow would be happy. Soon the butler arrived, and they asked him to pour them a 1920 Macallan whisky, a million euros a bottle. This was an occasion that merited it.

'*Vashe zdorovie*! (Cheers!)' Yuri said, raising his glass.

'*Vashe zdorovie*!'

After savouring the sweet nectar they had just been served, Yuri, with the relaxed confidence of a good friend, asked:

'What now?'

'I have to go home,' Moscow was his home, 'and report back.'

'And then, a holiday?'

Ivan looked exasperated. He allowed himself to show his feelings because Yuri was a close friend, someone he trusted completely and knew would be discrete.

'Something tells me no, Yuri. I'm afraid not. Our service was not created simply to turn us into art thieves. I know there's something behind this. Something very big. So big that I haven't been told about it yet. Maybe because I'm not responsible for what comes next.'

'Don't you have the slightest suspicion?'

'No. That's why I say it's something big, because you nearly always get some clue or hear a rumour or a hint from some direction. But on this occasion, there has been complete and utter secrecy. And I'm very much afraid they're going to ruin a well-earned holiday in Marbella.'

'When are we going home?'

'Tomorrow. Now I have to call to make arrangements. Tell the flight crew to get ready. We'll meet up later.'

'OK, see you later.'

***

Just as the yacht *Irina* raised looks of astonishment and curiosity, the private jet that Ivan used for his travels was a sight to behold on the runways of any airport.

It had a capacity for nineteen passengers, although most of the time, apart from the four crew members, Ivan travelled alone or with only a couple of people as companions.

Its dimensions were cyclopean for a private jet. Forty-four metres long, with a wingspan of thirty-two metres and a height of eight metres, it looked both imposing and yet at the same time sleek and lightweight. Its flight range allowed it to travel from Sydney to Chicago non-stop, at a speed of over nine hundred kilometres per hour, and at an altitude of thirteen thousand metres. It needed one thousand eight hundred metres for take-off and less than half that for landing.

The interior was equipped with every luxury and convenience, including a fully equipped kitchen that offered passengers a sumptuous menu wherever they went and a well-stocked bar to make the voyage even more comfortable. For longer trips, the aircraft boasted a spacious bedroom, complete with double bed and sitting area for privacy, as well as a lavishly decorated en suite bathroom.

Ivan and Yuri arrived at the airport on schedule. It had been organised with military precision. After complying with the legal formalities, they made their way to the aircraft and climbed the steps. At the top, the crew was waiting to welcome them. They chose two seats in the front row and made themselves comfortable. They had a seven-hour journey ahead of them to get back home.

The flight crew took up their positions. The two stewardesses sat down and the aircraft began taxiing prior to lift-off. The captain announced over the loudspeaker "Prepare for take-off" and everyone felt the power of the engines as they took it into a steep climb. Once the plane had stabilized and reached cruising altitude and speed, one of the stewardesses came over to ask if they'd like an alcoholic drink, a coffee or a fruit juice.

'I'll have a coffee, please,' said Ivan.

'Make that two, please.'

They had eaten a copious breakfast at Ivan's villa and there was no question of arriving at such an important meeting reeking of whisky. Not today.

Towards midday the stewardess returned to offer them the menu of dishes available on board. Given the time it would take to get there, plus the drive to FSB headquarters and the subsequent meeting, they needed to eat on the plane. Two Olivier potato salads and some beluga caviar was enough to satisfy their appetites, accompanied by a good Rioja Gran Reserva. All of the best quality that was available.

They had eaten and drunk to their hearts' content and there were still a few hours of flying ahead. So, Ivan opened his laptop to see if there was any news. And there was:

Too many leads uncovered. Interpol is investigating prints from stolen car. Card for the club Irina found in uniforms. Visit to club planned. Security company under suspicion. Hand-drawn maps under suspicion. Unidentified person ordered key. Yacht, soon to be under suspicion. In addition, someone has let the cat out of the bag and put the names of Grigori and Vasili on the table. WE HAVE A MOLE IN THE GARDEN. And there are still the mobile Sim cards.

It doesn't look good. The operation isn't looking very tidy. Too many loose ends.

"The mole", as always, had provided valuable information.

Ivan's worried face did not go unnoticed by Yuri.

'Is everything all right?'

Ivan thought about telling him the truth but opted for another answer.

'Everything's fine.'

If the aim was to reassure him, he hadn't succeeded.

After a long seven-hour flight, the plane landed at Moscow Domodedovo Airport and parked in the VIP area. At the bottom of the steps, the official car - a black Aurus Senat - was waiting to take them to the FSB headquarters. There, Ivan would meet his boss Dmitry Kuznetsov, the head of the security agency. It also seemed logical to assume that the president, Igor Ruskin, would be there. It would be to them that he would have to deliver the report on the operation.

Moscow was about forty-five kilometres north of the airport on the A-105 motorway.

A huge Neo-Baroque building with an imposing facade of yellow brick came into view in the distance. It was the FSB headquarters, better known by the infamous name of the Lubyanka, and as it drew nearer, the driver announced to his distinguished passengers

'We are arriving, sir.'

As the car drew up to the building, it took the side entrance, a much more discreet way in, which was reserved for the more exclusive visitors.

Getting out of the car and heading down the hallway towards the special lift that led to Kuznetsov's office, Ivan felt at home. He missed the corridors, the offices, the day-to-day routine of operations around the world. He suffered perhaps from Ulysses syndrome, so common amongst migrants, which led him to take refuge in the dissipated and extravagant lifestyle that he enjoyed so much in Monaco and especially in Marbella.

There, the Russian expat community could observe him close up and thus become a passive part of the spectacle.

Before the entrance to his boss's office there was a large waiting room where those who were to be received by Kuznetsov waited their turn. Yuri, without needing to be told, left Ivan to make his way through the doors which led to the official workplace of the chief of the FSB. He then sought out a comfortable velvet-lined seat and prepared to wait as long as it took for Ivan to emerge. Seven hours of flying and another hour and a half from the airport had tired him out. He laid his head down to rest for a moment and fell asleep. The snoring startled Kuznetsov's assistants and secretaries, who didn't know what to do. It was no surprise that they were nonplussed, they knew he held the rank of lieutenant colonel and was the right-hand man of Ivan Orlov, the all-powerful FSB agent and personal friend of the president, and whether out of fear, caution, compassion or a mixture of all of these, they let him enjoy his snooze.

Upon entering the office, Ivan was greeted like a hero by his boss, Dmitri Kuznetsov. Ivan thought this was a bit over the top, but he understood that his friendship with Igor, the president, put Dmitri himself in an awkward position. Nevertheless, Ivan maintained a respectful and considerate attitude towards him, as if he genuinely regarded him as his superior. Once inside, Kuznetsov led him to a more discreet inner room, where Igor Ruskin was waiting for him. Out of respect for them both, Ivan did not give him a hug, which was what they did in private. He merely shook his hand and nodded his head in a gesture of respect and recognition of his authority.

Sitting around a coffee table with gold legs and a marble top, they prepared to listen to Ivan's explanations of how the operation had progressed. But first, one of the secretaries approached and offered them something to eat from the buffet at the side of the room. Igor and Dimitri accepted, but Ivan said that he had already eaten lunch, although he could do with some coffee.

He then began to recount in detail how the theft of the artwork and its subsequent sale to the Qatari had progressed.

He explained that he had ensured collaboration both from the security company and the domestic staff of the gentleman who had been robbed, which helped to simplify matters. He went to great lengths to emphasise that despite the large group of people involved in the operation, including electronics specialists, no one knew the identities of the other members of the team. Those who carried out the robbery, for example, had been recruited by another FSB agent. The rest acted in the dark without knowing any details other than those that concerned each one. All of them had been motivated solely by money, and once they had received what they had agreed, communication was cut off. The compartmentalization strategy guaranteed discretion and ensured that the different groups were isolated from each other, which would effectively hamper the work of the police. In his view, the police had nothing, and if they did, it would be too little, too late and too disjointed. But, crucially, he chose not to share the inconvenient details that had been forwarded to his special email account a few hours ago.

'Nevertheless, we have heard that two individuals had to be eliminated,' Dmitri intervened tactfully, taking care not to offend either Ivan or the president.

'Yes, there was no choice. After they had agreed on the deal and on the amount they would be paid, greed got the better of them. They were dubious about the operation and demanded more money, and it would have been too risky to ignore it.'

'Of course, I understand,' said Dimitri, trying to support his man's decision and put the matter to rest. 'And the people who carried out the job don't represent a risk?' he suggested meekly.

'For a start, they are two missing links in a chain which they themselves know nothing about. And, besides, we can't go around littering the Costa del Sol with corpses, as if it were Chicago in the 1930s, can we?' Ivan replied, a little irritated.

Igor considered that the meeting had achieved its objective. He had been fully briefed and everything seemed to be clear. Now it was time for the second phase of the operation. And so it was he, Igor, who now intervened.

'Congratulations, Ivan. It was a superbly designed and executed operation.'

'Thank you, President.'

'But now there is another mission.'

'I am at your service, President.'

'I'm aware of that. That's why you have a new mission: to deliver a special cargo to the port of Magadan on the Sea of Okhotsk.'

In the arse end of nowhere, damn it! Ivan thought without moving a muscle.

'The goods are to be loaded and moved from that port to Hai Phong in Vietnam. We trust you to control and supervise the whole operation. It's of vital importance to your country.'

Ivan knew they weren't telling him everything. He wasn't an errand boy to be put in charge of regular everyday merchandise. For that, they'd send a warehouse boy. He felt manipulated and working in the dark, and he didn't like that, although he had to follow orders like the good soldier he was. But, more importantly, he felt he was too old for that kind of operation. There were people in his team who were perfectly capable of carrying out such a mission. Besides, for him it wouldn't mean much more kudos than he already had, but for a new, younger agent, it would be good for their career.

'Sir, I thank you for your confidence in me and I recognize its value, but I must be honest with you: I feel a little old for these adventures. I am close to seventy and I am not as strong as I was in my youth. The mission, in my humble opinion, needs someone with more vigour and, to be honest, more ambition. Someone for whom it would be a step forward in his career. I'm sorry to disappoint you and I hope you will forgive me.'

The president was not expecting such a response, but after a few moments of thought, he came to the conclusion that Ivan was right. It was going to be a mission that would require a great deal of physical effort due to the distances to be covered and the mode of transport to be used. It was going to be very demanding and very tough.

'You're right, Ivan. Throughout your career you have given an enormous service to your country and you deserve a rest. You are no longer... we are both no longer capable of inflicting such a pounding on our bodies. Even though we keep ourselves more or less fit. But it's one thing to practice judo in the gym and another to travel in a military plane, eight thousand kilometres and then take a boat trip. I thank you for your sincerity.'

Dimitri listened to this conversation between the two friends without batting an eyelid or saying a word. He didn't want to break the atmosphere of camaraderie yet he was astounded that an agent could contradict the president and still be alive to tell the tale.

'Who do you have in mind, Ivan?'

'Oleg Sokolov. He has my full support and confidence.'

'Well then, so be it,' Igor declared. 'Dimitri, send for our friend Oleg.'

'Yes, President.'

'Will you be present at the meeting?'

'Yes, of course.'

'Then I will organise it immediately.'

'Perfect. Thank you both very much.'

Then he got up and left Dmitri's office through a side door, leaving Dmitri with Ivan.

'What do you plan to do with yourself, Ivan?'

'As I said, I feel old. I'm almost seventy and I just want to relax. I'm very tired. It's been fifty years, Dimitri. Fifty years, for Christ's sake!'

'Yes. That's a long time. Too long. I think you've earned a decent retirement. Where are you going to go, Monte Carlo?'

'I think I'll settle in Marbella.'

'I wish you all the best, then,' said Dimitri, offering his hand as they rose from their seats.

'Thanks. Anyway, if I can still be of any help, you can count on me, but nothing too strenuous. Right now, I can't wait to get into bed and sleep for twelve hours solid.'

'So long, Ivan.'

'So long, Boss.'

19.   Daniel and the yacht *Irina*

Daniel was totally focused on pursuing the stolen picture, which, among other things, was the reason Bukowski had hired him. From experience he knew that, depending on the complications, the task could take him several years, something that, at the moment, worried him because he knew that his client, Bukowski, did not have unlimited time left to live. He felt burdened by the responsibility of knowing he was essential to its recovery and at the same time being under a time restriction. This wasn't the way he was used to working.

Once he had spoken to his friend Stefano in prison, he had to confirm the theory of the yacht and for that he went to the marina in Marbella.

There, Daniel had an outboard motorboat which he occasionally used for trips. Sometimes, when he was feeling particularly down, or bored, he would cruise aimlessly, without a goal. The pleasure of the wind, the sun, the sea and the salt freed him from his gloomy thoughts and when he returned to port he felt better. On other occasions he would entertain his friends and take them for a tour without straying too far from the coast.

He was not a close friend of the director of the marina, but they had met at some events in the port and at a couple of private parties. That was enough of an excuse for him to chat with him and to do so in an official capacity.

He was a little younger than Daniel and had an open, cordial, friendly character, although he had his detractors, as was to be expected in any political post.

On arriving at the port, Daniel went straight to the offices to see if by any luck he might be able to see him. He struck lucky.

The port director remembered - or so he said - that they had met at a party and, purely as a matter of routine, he checked that Daniel was up to date with his obligations as skipper of a boat moored there.

Daniel didn't beat about the bush and told him that he was assisting the police in the investigation of a robbery and that he needed his help. There is nothing more seductive for a politician, Daniel thought, than to be asked for help.

Moreover, the port director knew of Daniel's many contacts, friends and acquaintances and wasn't keen for the slightest rumour to circulate about his competence or willingness to cooperate. They were influential people and he didn't want to get into trouble with his political party.

Daniel asked if he could provide him with the list of boats that left Marbella in the early hours of the morning of the robbery, from 3am onwards. The director went to the port's database and verified that on that night and at that time, there was only one yacht that left the port. Her name was *Irina*. He also provided Daniel with all the information he needed relating to it: the owner, the ship's flag, the country of registration, and most importantly, the destination.

After that meeting, as agreed, Daniel contacted Frutos and brought him up to date. He then had another discussion with Bukowski. In it, he informed him of the lead he had to follow that would take him, initially, to Monaco, even though it was clear that there was no guarantee of success.

'You must go, Daniel. You must go. And carry on with your work. I'm aware that there's nothing in the way of guarantees, but that can't be a reason for not going. When do you plan to leave?'

'Well, I'll have to book a flight and find accommodation.'

'Never mind all that. Have you forgotten that I have a private jet?'

'I didn't consider that, sir.'

'And don't you know that I own one of the best hotels in Monaco?'

'I didn't know that either.'

'It's the Hotel Ambassador Imperator. Well, that problem is solved. You have your flight and hotel. All you have to do is tell me when you plan to leave, so I can let the crew know and have everything ready.'

'Give me two days to make arrangements.'

'So, the day after tomorrow?'

'If it's not too much of a rush for the crew, that's perfect for me.'

'All right, then. Consider it done.'

'Thank you very much, Mr Bukowski'.

'One more thing.'

'Yes.'

'When you get to the hotel, give me a call. Without fail.'

'Of course. I'll do that. And thanks again.'

'Good luck, Mr Olavarría, or should I call you Don Daniel,' he said with a mischievous grin.

***

It was not the first time Daniel had boarded a private plane, but it was the first time he had flown on a jet belonging to the client he was working for.

In addition, Bukowski had insisted on sending his chauffeur driven car to take him to the airport, and Daniel could not refuse such a kind gesture. No doubt his client was making the most of this part of his life. Daniel realized that you could easily get used to such a luxurious way of life, as long as you had the fortitude to put up with having a precious piece of art stolen from you.

He said goodbye to the chauffer at the foot of the steps and before he knew it, a member of the crew had collected his bags and was carrying them up to the cabin. As he passed through the cabin door, he greeted the captain and the rest of the crew and settled down to enjoy the flight, which was to last a couple of hours. Once he was in his seat, one of the flight attendants asked him if he was ready. He confirmed he was and almost immediately the take-off manoeuvres began. As soon as they were in the air, the hostess offered him a drink and Daniel opted for a coffee.

During the flight he had plenty of time to reflect on how the case was progressing.

The modus operandi of the thieves did not correspond to anything he had seen before, which made it even more difficult to identify the perpetrators. In addition, the two security guards had been killed. He had no leads other than the remote possibility that the yacht *Irina* was involved, but even so, when he arrived in Monaco he would have to delve deep beneath the surface to see if he could uncover something more. Monaco was certainly not a bastion of sanctity. Many of its residents were there solely because of the things they had to hide, but perhaps because of that, people tended to keep their mouths shut. He certainly had an arduous task ahead of him, one of the most difficult he had faced in his long career, and he did not want to abuse his client's good nature. As time went on, he found he had more and more respect for the man and was growing increasingly fond of him.

He tried to go through the sources he could turn to for information and how he could contact them. Normally, those type of people were not to be found in the phone book. He would start with those with whom he was in regular contact, even if it was only by email or on social networks. And he should not forget his client's offer.

All of a sudden, the 'fasten your seat belts' warning flashed on, and he heard the captain announce that the aircraft would be arriving in a few minutes and that they should prepare for landing.

After touching down and taxiing along the runway to a hangar in the zone reserved for private jets, the engines shut down. Daniel had arrived in Nice. From there, he would leave for the hotel in Monaco.

20.   Vasili and Grigori remain in hiding

Ever since the day Vasili saw the television pictures of the two of them on the night of the robbery, his mind had been in turmoil. Maybe someone had recognised them. Maybe it was in someone's interest to eliminate them.

When he saw it on TV, he didn't say anything to Grigori because he knew he would get really agitated and, worst of all, he wouldn't come up with a solution to the problem. It was a habit of his that Vasili by now knew all too well. But he himself couldn't stop thinking about it.

Vasili felt that it was one thing to commit a robbery, but quite another to be accused of murder. That was a serious matter. They might well be called petty criminals, small time crooks, racketeers, pickpockets, even thugs, but premeditated killing was something else entirely. At best, after some time, you might be able to prove that you had nothing to do with it, but from the start you would be in prison, awaiting trial and without much hope of either staying alive or regaining your freedom. They were foreigners, Russians - not all of whom had a good reputation - and they were accused of robbery and murder. No jury would acquit them. How on earth could they prove that they had never fired a shot, that they had no weapons, that they knew nothing about the security guards nor that they were the ones that they were replacing on the residential estate? How could they prove that they had been hired by a man called Oleg, if that was indeed his real name, who may not even still be in Spain? He even considered the possibility that, when they were brought to trial, some fake witness like Oleg, or the waitress, or anyone else in his pay, could come forward, claiming to have witnessed the crime or seen them buy the guns or provide some other information that would incriminate them. This way,

Oleg's people - he dreaded to think who they were - would make sure they went to prison and once inside, someone would eliminate them so there would be no loose ends. The truth is that Vasili began to see it all under a very black cloud. Or at least, a dark grey one.

For the first time for many years they felt proud of themselves. They had found honest jobs that allowed them to live reasonably, in the pleasant town of Rota, a small place but one that had everything, including a fantastic beach where they spent long hours in the sun, or exercising along the shore, playing football when there was no one around, or running along the promenade. They had got used to their new life, their new home.

The boss was a good man who treated them with respect and paid them every month. They lived in a decent, modern flat that was very comfortable and they even paid a lady to clean the house, sharing the cost between them. They slept in clean sheets in real beds, not bunk beds or straw mattresses and had a bathroom with hot water. For the first time in ages they didn't have to break anyone's legs, or beat them up, or rob a bank to earn some money, never knowing how long that money would last.

They got up early to go to work, carried out their assigned tasks, finished and had time off to have a beer, enjoy the warm weather, the beach and some pretty girls. They didn't need to visit whores as they always had before.

They had met two girls at a bar in the village one Friday night. They were friendly and pretty and didn't care that they were foreigners and worked as construction workers. The girls were impressed by how big they were whilst at the same time they thought they were like cuddly teddy bears. For the boys, it was the girls' friendliness and easy-going manner. Both girls also worked, one in a health food shop and the other in a supermarket. The four of them enjoyed each other's company, they laughed at the language differences, the blunders the boys made in Spanish, their accents and some of their expressions.

They felt free, as if no one was chasing them, and it worried Vasili - a lot - to think of the possibility that all that could disappear overnight. And moreover, because of something they hadn't done. It was true: they had become part of the bourgeoisie, but he had discovered that there was nothing wrong with that. It was then that he began to think of a more or less graceful way out.

One day when the two of them were alone on the beach enjoying the last rays of sunshine of the day, Vasili blurted out to his friend everything he had been ruminating on since the day they arrived. He didn't tell him about the TV so as not to alarm him but tried to make him understand that the best option they had was to turn themselves in to the police and confess to the robbery. Tell them the whole story and try to negotiate a deal in exchange for protection. They didn't have much information, but between choosing to trust the police or to trust Oleg and his heavies, Vasili was in no doubt. If they didn't, they ran the risk of being caught off guard by either one or the other in the near future when they least expected it. He figured it was better to go ahead and take the bull by the horns. He thought it would give them a better chance of negotiating.

There was also another reason and he ended up confessing it to his friend. Vasili was falling in love with the girl he was dating. She was the kind of person who makes you want to be better. He knew he didn't deserve her and that he had to tell her the truth if he was ever to do so. He was starting to feel uncomfortable that he couldn't tell her his whole story. He didn't want there to be any deception or lies between them, or worse still, for example, that they might get married and then suddenly he was shot in the head or put in handcuffs. That was another reason for him to be honest with the girl. He was serious about her. It was the first time anyone had ever shown him affection without money being involved. And for that he was going to have the courage to confess everything to her and pray that she wouldn't run away. She would be within her rights, but Vasili couldn't manipulate her feelings by withholding the truth, by deceiving her. But in order to do all that, he needed to talk it over with his friend and get his opinion. And that's what he was doing: laying his cards on the table.

Grigori looked at him in astonishment and silence. He looked at him as if to say, "So you've been thinking about all that since we arrived and that's why you had that worried look on your face. Now I understand it all." What surprised him most was the confession that he was falling in love with the girl. He too had fallen in love with the lass from the supermarket, but he didn't have the courage to talk to her and confess his feelings, let alone tell his friend. He felt ashamed. And yet, if Vasili were to tell his girlfriend, clearly his own had to know about it too. That's when Grigori really started to be afraid. He was more frightened of the girl's reaction than of any henchmen Oleg or the police themselves might send them. The Spanish police were not dangerous when compared to those in Moscow or in some of the many eastern countries they had drifted through before coming to rest on the Costa del Sol.

Both were sitting on their respective beach towels on the sand. Grigori had been listening to his friend, with his legs stretched out and supported by his hands behind him. When Vasili finished his long speech, he tucked his legs into the lotus position and let his gaze wander to the horizon. In the distance, he could see a huge cargo ship, loaded to the brim with containers leaving the port of Cadiz, and over their heads, far away above the sea, they saw and heard a military helicopter from the naval base. A respectful silence fell between them. Grigori, at last, showed signs of composure and calm. He was weighing up everything his friend had said. Vasili, in turn, wanted to give his friend time to reflect on the situation and didn't want to rush him. Finally, after a long pause, when the sun was almost setting over the horizon, Grigori plucked up the courage to say:

'Vasili, you've forgotten about Sofia.'

'No, I haven't. But you have to choose the lesser of two evils. It's one thing to take the rap for something we did at the time, a long time ago, but we did it, and another to take the rap for something we didn't do, like killing two people. And besides, as soon as we're out in the open, Oleg's thugs will be happy to send us to the bottom of the sea in concrete shoes.'

Grigori thought for a few moments. He had a worried look on his face, and rightly so. But he had to accept that his friend was right. Finally, he broke the silence.

'What if the girls tell us to go fuck ourselves?'

Vasili didn't reply. Grigori, too, remained silent.

21.   The police now have plenty of leads to follow

Inspector Navarro's enquiries regarding the yachts that may have sailed in the early hours of the day of the robbery bore fruit. It was confirmed that there was a yacht, the *Irina*, which was the same yacht as the one suspected by Daniel. And the trail led to Monaco. From then on, he had to stand back and leave the investigation to others. Navarro could go no further.

The request for information from Interpol had also been worthwhile.

The fingerprints found inside the getaway car belonged to two Russians who had been arrested in Bulgaria for bank robbery a few years earlier. A robbery without casualties or injuries and for a ridiculous amount. Afterwards, they managed to flee the country by bribing the guards who were taking them to prison. Their names were Grigori Utkin and Vasili Konstantinov. In Spain they had behaved well and were never arrested.

Perhaps it was no coincidence that those were the same names that an anonymous female voice with an eastern accent had left on the voicemail when they had got the press involved.

They had found a card from the nightclub *Irina la Dulce* in one of the uniforms left in the getaway car.

As soon as Interpol sent them the photographs of the two men, Frutos ordered Encinas and his team to check out the nightclub.

They spoke to the manager, who was also Russian and said his name was Oleg. He told them he had never seen the men before in his life. They asked the waitresses and they were all uncooperative and very reticent. It was clear that they were frightened and could not speak freely. All except one.

They left the club conscious that they would return sooner or later. For the time being, there were other lines of investigation.

Now that they knew their identities, had obtained photographs and had checked the data on the Sim cards, it was a simple matter to find out where they lived.

Encinas and his group went there, with the idea of questioning them. When they got there, they showed the photographs to the caretaker. He recognized them but said that he hadn't heard from them for some time, he hadn't seen them or heard any noise from inside the house.

As there was no lift, they walked up to the third floor in order to interrogate them. They knocked several times but nobody opened the door and there was no noise from within. Drawing their weapons as a precaution, they decided to enter, covered by the search warrant that Encinas – cautious as ever - was carrying in his pocket.

They forced the lock and Encinas, on his guard, opened it very slowly while pointing his pistol at whatever might be waiting for them. The other two officers stood behind him.

The living room was lit by natural light. The furnishings were minimalist: a sofa, a dining table with a few chairs and a piece of furniture on top of which there was a TV.

A small, American-style kitchen greeted them to the left of the entrance. Everything seemed empty and silent.

They advanced carefully and silently down the short corridor that appeared to lead to the bedrooms. There were two. Both were empty and untidy.

'There is no one here, sir.'

'Yes, so it seems.'

'Sir, there's rotten food in the fridge. It smells awful.'

Encinas began to piece things together: the bedrooms were a mess, the beds unmade, lots of clothes in the wardrobe, food and beers in the fridge, the house empty, no signs of a struggle, no evidence of blood anywhere.

'Everything indicates that they left in a hurry and have no plans to return,' Encinas said out loud. 'Now we need to find out where they are... if they're still alive. Search around and see if we can find anything of interest.'

'What are we looking for, sir?'

'I really don't know. Anything that might help us know if they are alive or where they are.'

The three of them rummaged around for more than an hour in the vain attempt to find some clue.

'We're not going to find anything here. Let's go.'

As they headed downstairs, the caretaker seemed very interested in trying to glean information to promptly pass on to the rest of the block, in the hope of increasing his standing amongst the neighbours and becoming someone important.

'What can you tell us about these two, Vasili and Grigori?'

'What I told you before. They are good people. Kind, polite. They don't create problems. No quarrels, no fights.'

'Any visitors?'

'Not that I know of, but I only work certain hours. I don't know if they see anyone at night. The neighbours certainly haven't complained.'

'Is there anything that has happened lately that you consider special or out of the ordinary?'

The man thought for a few moments before answering.

'No. Nothing that I can remember.'

'Who cleaned their house?'

'No one. They prefer to do it themselves. They're just simple people, I don't suppose their salary is enough for them to splash out.'

'Do you know the name of the owner of the flat?'

'An English guy. The rental is handled by an agency, but since they rented it, they haven't been here. I know these two pay every month, on the nail. They're Russian and they take things like that very seriously.'

'Do you know what work they were doing?'

'No, sir. But I think they did a bit of everything. Sometimes chauffeur, sometimes bodyguard, you know, a bit of this and a bit of that. They made a living.'

'Do you know if they were security guards in any particular company?'

'No idea, sir.'

'If they didn't have a steady job, where did they get the money to live, pay the bills, pay for food...?'

'I imagine from the same place as anyone else in the same situation, sir.'

'Fine. You've been very helpful. Here's my card. If you remember anything, even if it seems trivial or unimportant, please don't fail to call me, OK?'

'Yes, sir. I will.'

Encinas and his group gave up their attempt to contact the security guards.

There was another avenue of investigation left to pursue: the shift manager of the security company.

After his secret informant pointed to the shift manager as an accomplice - at least - in the robbery, Encinas had to subject him to some tough questioning.

He sent a patrol car to pick him up and take him to the police station.

Without his help, it would have been an unacceptable risk for the perpetrators of the robbery to even approach the security checkpoint at the residential estate. The only way the substitution of the two guards could have gone unnoticed was by a breach of trust on his part.

Encinas and a couple of his assistants took turns to break the manager's spirit. He knew that his confession meant losing his job and in a world where trust was everything, the only thing left for him to do would be to become a nightclub bouncer or a bodyguard for some thug.

For two days and after countless hours of interrogation, Encinas managed to instil the fear of God into him.

'We know it was you who made the fake ID cards. You were identified by a waitress at the nightclub.'

The security guard's face reflected his shock. The bluff worked.

'But that's not the most serious thing. The most serious thing is that that night, you turned a blind eye to allow access to two individuals who were not the usual guards. And they weren't the usual ones because you yourself had killed them.'

'No! No way! I didn't know they were going to be killed! I swear! It wasn't me!'

'Then tell me what you knew and maybe I won't accuse you of being an accessory to murder.'

That's when the exhausted security guard, backed into a corner, finally cracked.

'They only told me I had to make some ID cards. Nobody told me anything about killing anybody, I swear! I knew those guys. They were good people. When I found out, I thought they'd come after me next.'

'How much did they pay you?'

The guard had now completely lost it and was sobbing pathetically. He was ashamed of himself and scared to death of how complicated things had become.

'Ten thousand. Five thousand for each one.'

'Who paid you?'

'The manager of the nightclub. Well, a huge bouncer who didn't fit into his suit and had no neck, but I knew he worked for him.'

'Do you know what the manager's name is?'

'Oleg.'

'Who actually made the cards?'

'I did them myself. Sometimes, when we are short of staff and we need them urgently, there isn't time to send the request to the printer to have them made. So, when one of the guards is on sick leave or simply leaves without warning and we need to find a replacement, the shift managers have the appropriate material to make them themselves. Without the bosses' knowledge, but we do it.'

'Where did you do it?'

'In the back room of the nightclub.'

And that's how the previously unknown Grigori and Vasili got theirs.

Encinas now had another witness against Oleg. The other was secret and could not be exposed.

He left the interrogation room and told the officer guarding the door,

'Take him away and book him. Charge him with accessory to

robbery and membership of a criminal gang.'

Encinas thought he had enough evidence to go after this Oleg and bring him in to the police station. But now they also had a statement from someone implicated in the crime, which established that the fake ID cards were made at the club.

He requested a meeting with Frutos to bring him up to date and ask for the go-ahead.

'Sir,' insisted Encinas. 'We should go back to the club and arrest this Oleg. With the lies he has told us together with the shift manager's statement, we have more than enough to bring him in to interrogate him.'

After a few moments of reflection, Frutos replied:

'It's still a bit premature, Encinas. I don't want him to give us the slip and it could be a defensive ploy on the part of the security guard manager. We must wait a little longer.'

Encinas could not believe what he was hearing. It seemed impossible that the superintendent could be so hesitant and maintain that it was not yet clear what should be done. He didn't agree at all with such caution, but it was the superintendent who was in charge. If Frutos wanted more evidence, he would follow up on other lines of enquiry.

They also visited the club where the men were allegedly seen spending lots of money, although they were not regulars. The waiters were struck by the fact that they didn't know them at all, yet they were very generous and treated the girls with respect, which was probably why they remembered them.

The police returned to the establishment and when they showed the photographs, even though they were old ones, the waiters recognised them.

'Yes, that's them. They ordered the best bottle of vodka and then a couple of girls. They treated them well, paid for everything without complaint and left without making a fuss, which doesn't always happen.'

'Do you remember roughly when that was?'

'That's tricky. About two or three weeks ago?'

That would mean it was BEFORE the robbery. For the dates to fit, they must have visited the club after they were given some sort of advance on the money. A couple of hard-up guys, with no steady job and looking for work, don't end the night in a nightclub asking for the most expensive bottle of vodka and two prostitutes unless they've got their hands on some cash. And the only explanation Encinas found was that they had been given an advance for the job.

What the police officers were most encouraged by, and what offered them the most leads, was the recovery of the micro SD cards from the phones. Initially they had no evidence that these cards, found on the ground in the vicinity of the stolen getaway car, belonged to the suspects, but they had to check. They had to rely on companies specialising in the recovery of severely damaged devices and eventually they were successful.

The head of telecoms called Encinas to give him an update.

'Inspector, we have restored the data on the SD cards from the mobiles.'

'You lot are awesome! I'm on my way there now.'

When he arrived at the lab, he sat down next to the officer who had called him, a young man in his early twenties, but a real tec whizz.

'What have you got for me, Wizard?'

'The names of the owners. They're Russian.'

'Someone named Vasili and the other Grigori?'

'Christ! What do you need me for, Inspector?'

'What else?'

'We can retrieve all the calls, their origin, time and all the associated data. We can also trace the phones and if they're in someone's name, identify them.'

'Brilliant. Can you let me have all those details?'

'Do you want it in Excel?'

'Yes, that would be great.'

Once Encinas had copied the data onto a USB key, he went to his desk to study the information. When he discovered certain facts that he considered relevant, he requested another meeting with Frutos.

'Sir, starting from the date shown on the report that the getaway car was stolen, I have been trying to establish a link with one of the telephone numbers on the list. Presumably, whoever stole the car called them to deliver it to them. They must have come to some arrangement. Either that, or Vasili and Grigori stole the car themselves. But I needed to confirm my theory. There's a number that could be suspect. Later I'll ask the tec guys to give me the name of the owner, if possible.'

Frutos listened attentively while Encinas continued:

'If it turns out that someone else stole the car, perhaps by tracing back, we might be able to find out who ordered it to be taken. That's how professionals normally work, at least, and it seems clear that this was a professional job.

Analysing the Excel files that "the Wizard" gave me, I also found it very interesting that both phones had calls from another number which I later found out was in the name of the *Irina* nightclub.

Once again, repeatedly, that same nightclub comes up, sir.'

At this point, Encinas stopped his story and scrutinised Frutos' face to see if he could discover any reaction. Nothing. It was the impenetrable face. So, he continued with his report.

'It is clear to me, sir, that another visit to this goddamn club is becoming urgent.'

He paused again to see if Frutos would make another comment intended to stall the investigation. But the superintendent had remained silent.

Encinas thought that maybe it was because Frutos himself frequented the place and didn't want it to be known. Be that as it may, they needed to pay another visit to the manager, but this time they would have to bring him in to the police station for a more private chat. There were too many links and too many lies.

'There's more, sir. Most importantly, on the night of the murder of the two security guards, neither of the two phones belonging to Vasili and Grigori were even remotely close to either of the two murder sites. The telecom guys confirmed this to me. And they didn't turn them off either. They were switched on and didn't move away from their homes.'

As Encinas concluded his lengthy report, he was surprised at the lack of enthusiasm from Frutos. To Encinas, it seemed as though at last things were starting to move, after several days in which they appeared to have ground to a halt.

Frutos called Navarro and the others into the meeting room for a briefing.

'Gentlemen, we have made good progress. I'll give you a quick overview. We have the particulars of the yacht *Irina* and are reasonably certain that it was the means used by the thieves to transport the picture to Monte Carlo. And our collaborator, Daniel Olavarría, has also confirmed this.'

And he continued:

'We've got the insider from the security company responsible for forging the cards and turning a blind eye to the two thieves. He's already in custody.

We have the phone numbers of those who executed the robbery. We've confirmed where they're from.

We need to talk to the nightclub manager again, this Oleg guy. Encinas,' he said, looking at his homicide inspector, 'bring him in to the station, OK?'

'Yes Chief.'' *At last, damn it!* he thought.

'And while you're at it, bring in that waitress too. I have a feeling she knows something and if we bring her boss in, maybe she'll talk.'

'Her attitude was different, Chief, as if she had a special status among the waitresses. Her name was Marina Smolensk.'

'Ok. The pieces of the puzzle are gradually fitting together. But there are still a few more loose ends and mysteries to be unravelled. For instance, where are these two Russians, Grigori and Vasili? Are they still alive? We also have to establish who the woman was who ordered the copy of the house key and how it was possible that the butler didn't realise that it had been taken.'

He went on:

'Apart from the key, someone on the inside had drawn up a plan of the layout of the house so that the thieves could move around without risk and find where the picture was hanging.

I still have a few questions that need answering: Who chose that particular picture and not another? The same person who provided the key? A stranger? Who knew it was there?'

Just at that moment, someone knocked on the door and announced:

'Superintendent, you have a phone call.'

'Not now, I'm just finishing.'

'I think it's urgent, sir.'

'Who is it?'

'Someone who says he has information about the robbery'.

Everyone in the room was shocked by the news.

'Put the call through to this number, please.'

'Right away, sir.'

The phone in the briefing room rang only once and Frutos reluctantly picked it up. He was convinced it was a crank and a waste of time.

'Chief Superintendent Frutos here, who am I speaking to?'

Those present watched as the expression of the poker-faced superintendent, famous for his inscrutable countenance, was transformed in seconds.

'How can I reach you?'

The response from the other end of the line went unheard. Frutos hung up the phone. His face was a genuine reflection of alarm, doubt, surprise and disbelief.

'Is something wrong, Chief?' Encinas asked.

'Gentlemen. The Russians who carried out the theft of the picture are alive.'

'Maybe it's a hoax, sir.'

'The man who just called me says his name is Vasili Konstantinov.'

***

This time what he wrote in his personal diary read:

Burglars identified. The shift manager of the security company has confessed his collaboration implicating the club. Sim cards analysed. Car thief identified. Calls from club to thieves. Thieves ruled out as killers. **Vasili and Grigori are negotiating to hand themselves in. <u>Arrest of Oleg is imminent</u>.**

22.   Daniel in Monaco

Arriving in Nice, Daniel descended the steps of Bukowski's private jet to find a car - a gleaming black Rolls Royce - waiting on the tarmac, courtesy of his client. As soon as he set foot on the ground, the chauffeur, in his immaculate grey uniform and matching peaked cap, hurried over to collect his bags and pay his respects.

'Welcome to Nice, Monsieur.'

'Thank you very much. What a splendid reception, but who are you?'

'Monsieur Bukowski sends his regards and asks you to be so kind as to accept a transfer to the heliport. It's the quickest and most comfortable option. There, a helicopter will take you to Monaco in less than ten minutes. By road it is a 45-minute drive.'

'OK, I accept with great pleasure.'

You have to admit, Daniel thought as he got into the car, *that Bukowski certainly has an eye for detail and knows how to live in style. No question about it.*

In just a couple of minutes they had reached the heliport, from where there was a flight to Monaco every quarter of an hour. In fact, one was just about to leave.

The chauffeur jumped out of the car, quickly picked up Daniel's luggage and encouraged him to follow him at a brisk pace the few metres to the helicopter. The chauffeur put the bags into the luggage rack of the helicopter then bade him farewell with a military salute, as it would have been impossible to make himself heard over the roar of the engine. A few seconds after sitting down with three other passengers and fastening his seatbelt, Daniel was in the air again.

It was certainly being quite an experience, this trip. He hoped he would be equally lucky in his investigations.

The seven minutes it took to reach Monaco's heliport seemed to pass by in seconds. As he stepped out of the aircraft, he was again met by a driver who, without needing to ask, appeared to recognise him.

> 'Monsieur Olavarría,' he said in a thick French accent, 'if you will allow me, I will be delighted to drive you to the hotel. Could you let me know which suitcases are yours, please?'

Ten minutes later he finally arrived at the hotel.

The building was magnificent, with a majestic, regal elegance. It was a reflection of a glamour and lifestyle more suited to a bygone age, but nevertheless, it was impressive. From an architectural point of view, it was a veritable jewel of the Belle Époque. The hotel was famous for its imposing glass dome designed by Gustave Eiffel himself.

As Daniel walked up to the reception desk, the manager greeted him with an exquisite French accent:

> 'Welcome, Monsieur Olavarría. It's a pleasure to have you with us, thank you for choosing us for your stay in our city. I hope that the imperial suite we have prepared for you will be to your liking, sir. If there's anything you're not happy with, please let us know immediately.'
>
> 'Thank you very much. You're very kind. I'm sure everything will be perfect.'
>
> 'I hope so, Monsieur. *Garçon! Veuillez prendre les bagages et escorter Monsieur à la suite impériale. Vite, vite!*'

The porter accompanied him to the top floor where the imperial suite was located. A lift for the sole use of its guests maintained that sense of exclusivity that the hotel wished to convey throughout the stay, while at the same time providing discretion for its most illustrious guests, from politicians to opera singers, rock stars to footballers.

Once inside, the waiter put the suitcases down and went to draw the curtains to let in the natural light. As he did so, a tsunami of light flooded the room, filling it with warmth. Daniel thought the suite was probably bigger than his entire flat in Marbella.

The suite was located in a corner of the building and the view of the deep blue water of the Mediterranean stretched all the way to the horizon. Two huge French windows, at right angles to each other and with glass from floor to ceiling, gave access to a terrace, partially covered by a porch. It was furnished in a modern style with extremely comfortable looking chairs, perfect for enjoying the magnificent spectacle on offer.

Daniel had been so impressed by the accommodation that he had forgotten about the poor porter who had helped him with his luggage, and the boy stood there, watching, somewhat perplexed, as the gentleman appeared overwhelmed. As soon as it dawned on him, he apologised and gave him a twenty-euro tip.

As soon as the porter had left the room, Daniel set about investigating his suite, primarily so that he wouldn't get lost in it one day and have to call for help.

The furniture in the main salon consisted of several leather chesterfields in delicate pale colours, around a low glass table with a cherry wood base. On it an ice bucket with a bottle of Krug champagne, bathed in ice, welcomed him, along with a card from the hotel management.

After inspecting the space where he was to reside, he felt it necessary to call Bukowski to thank him for all his attentions.

'Mr Bukowski?'

'Daniel, my friend! What a pleasure to hear from you. I imagine you have already arrived in Monaco and have been looked after as you deserve by our hotel staff.'

'Yes, I have. I am here enjoying all the luxuries that life has to offer, as a result of your generosity and hospitality. I wanted to thank you for all this.'

'*Carpe diem*, my friend Daniel. *Carpe diem*. I have learned that in the space of a minute you can lose everything. The tangible and the intangible. The works of art and the affection of your parents, siblings, friends and family. So enjoy it while you can.'

'I intend to.'

'Welcome to our hotel. I hope everything is to your liking.'

'Everything's perfect and the room is magnificent.'

'If you need anything at all, don't hesitate to contact me. And call when you have any news, OK?'

'You can count on it, sir.'

'Have a pleasant stay.'

'Thank you very much. We'll keep in touch.'

Bukowski, Daniel thought, did not fit the mould of the close-fisted multimillionaire he had so often seen. He had met many in his life, people with immense wealth, who then skimped on their employees' salaries or argued over the bill in the restaurants or jewellers they frequented. They complained endlessly about supposedly poor service or product quality, with the sole aim of making themselves more important than they were, intimidating the staff and, above all, demanding a discount.

They thought that by being inflexible, uncompromising, cantankerous, and severe, the people who served them would respect them more and pay them more attention, when in fact, what they were achieving was the opposite. Bukowski was certainly the antithesis of that.

He was a generous man who treated all his associates, his friends – the few he had - and his professional contacts with the utmost dignity and respect. It made no difference to Bukowski whether that person was a hotel porter, the manager or the owner. And that aspect of his character touched Daniel deeply.

At the beginning of this extraordinary job, he had been motivated by professional reasons, yes, but above all by pecuniary interests. Deep down, he loved to meet these Scrooge-like men, parsimonious types who enjoyed cheating people out of their money and even taking the bathrobes from hotels, simply because they thought they were within their rights because they had already paid for them. He liked to get an outrageous amount of money for his work, by charging them an indecent commission, which he knew would sting the reprobate millionaire. In general, this attitude was reserved solely for that type, as a punishment, since otherwise, in his more habitual environment, with those who did not indulge in this compulsive behaviour, his conduct was completely the opposite. In fact, he had earned a well-established reputation as a fair, honest and unbiased professional.

But in this particular case, his prejudices had blinded his judgement regarding Bukowski. He had at least realised this in time and was glad of it.

It was a beautiful day, the sun was shining, and he was in Monaco. Despite the speed with which he had flown there from Marbella by private jet, the truth was that he didn't feel like going out and wandering around the city. He preferred to stay in the hotel and eat there. Just before going down to the hotel restaurant for lunch, he made a mental inventory of the people he had to see.

First on the list was an individual who was considered to be the scum of the earth in the art world. But sometimes it is precisely that sort of scum that you have to deal with. His name: Edwin van Antwerp.

23.   Ivan Orlov retires to Marbella

After his refusal to lead the new mission, Ivan had managed to convince the president of the republic to grant him a kind of golden retirement. In return, he had to propose a replacement who offered the same guarantees of success as his own. That is how Oleg's name came up.

Oleg Sokolov was Ivan's right-hand man in the FSB hierarchy on the Costa del Sol. He was a disciplined and efficient agent, and when circumstances required it, ruthless. When he was given a mission there was no human being who could stop him from carrying it out. He was a missile without a self-destruct button. Ivan trusted him. He had known him for a long time and he had always performed to his full satisfaction, so he was sure that this time would be no different. He was also well connected on the Costa del Sol, where the *Irina* nightclub served as a cover for his activities and also gave him contacts with very influential people who had too much to hide, something that, for a spy, was a gold mine.

On the occasion of Oleg's professional promotion and his imminent change of residence, albeit temporary, Ivan wanted to organise a farewell party at his impressive mansion in Marbella. This was a magnificent villa on the top of a cliff overlooking the sea, with eight bedrooms, each with its own bathroom, constructed on three thousand square metres with five thousand square metres of surrounding land, where he could give free rein to his extravagance with tropical paradise gardens and a large neoclassical fountain that greeted you as soon as you entered the property.

Once inside the villa, a grand lobby, with a double ceiling, led into the main hall that opened onto the veranda, where one could enjoy a breath-taking view of the ocean. The separate dining room connected to a large kitchen.

The house had several guest suites - the smallest was sixty square metres - and a lift serving all floors of the palatial villa. The top level had a solarium with an incredible marble and stone mosaic floor and offered panoramic vistas of the ocean and the mountains.

In the basement there was a heated indoor swimming pool of eighty square metres, a Turkish bath, showers, bathroom, a gymnasium, a cinema and a temperature-controlled wine cellar. The area also included several storage rooms, a pump room and a service area.

Ivan decided to organise a lavish party for two reasons. The main, official reason was Oleg's promotion and his transfer to Moscow to receive instructions for his new "occupation". Ostensibly, he would be stepping down from the role of nightclub manager to take on other tasks at the company's headquarters in the capital. The second reason was Ivan's own retirement, which would be portrayed outwardly as a gradual - but inexorable - retirement from his multiple duties as Ukrainian Consul in Monaco and would entail longer periods of time spent in Marbella. He said he found Monaco too small, even claustrophobic.

For the organisation of the party and all the details he contacted a specialised events company called *Destellos Marbella*, whose role was to provide a network for Russian-speaking residents and tourists in Spain - almost half a million of them - and facilitate the integration of their social, family and business life into the local community through a wide range of communication platforms.

The company also offered consultancy services as a communications and advertising agency for those companies and organisations wishing to enter or strengthen their presence in the lucrative market of Russian clients.

He wanted it organised perfectly, in every detail. He gave precise instructions and one of his assistants called the company to hire their services. The company agreed to send one of its employees to review the facilities and the venue and to determine the client's wishes.

The company's representative requested a personal meeting with the host of the party to get to know first-hand his tastes, his preferences and something of his personality. Ivan gladly accepted the meeting and waited for her sitting comfortably in an armchair in the veranda on the first floor, enjoying the sea, while drinking his favourite whisky, Macallan.

Arriving at the villa, she was not particularly surprised by the place, although to anyone unaccustomed to such things it would be hard not to be impressed by the surroundings.

She rung the bell and an impeccably dressed butler led her through to where Ivan was waiting. She was greeted by an elderly gentleman, though later, when she learned his age, she had to admit that he looked younger.

The woman was experienced in dealing with people, especially with her fellow Russians, and she could see that, beneath that superficial layer of good manners and exquisite taste, there was a heart as hard and cold as steel. Just as hard and cold as the blue of his eyes.

He offered her something to drink and she asked for tea. From the outset she began to take notes and also, with Ivan's express permission, to record the conversation. She didn't want to miss any detail and Ivan liked that. She was methodical, conscientious and professional. She would have made a great spy, not least because of her beauty.

After an hour or so, she considered that she had everything she needed and she concluded the meeting. It was agreed that in two or three days she would submit a proposal with the estimated cost and if it was accepted, they would proceed accordingly.

24.   The Police, Vasili and Grigori

The unexpected call to the police station from Vasili, a prime suspect in the robbery and murders, left both the superintendent and his entire team completely perplexed. Encinas was a little less surprised because his informant had already tipped him off a few days earlier.

From the very moment Frutos hung up the phone, a brainstorming session was organised to try to figure out what the real purpose of the call was. Encinas preferred to listen rather than participate actively.

The first question to be answered was whether the man who phoned was really this Vasili as he claimed to be. It could be a ploy by someone else involved to waste the police's time while Vasili and perhaps his friend Grigori were resting in eternal sleep somewhere. Or maybe one of them killed the other and now wanted to blame the dead man.

After listening to various theories, some more plausible than others, Frutos pretty much passed judgement:

'What if it were true?'

They all remained silent, considering the question.

'What if it turns out that this Vasili wants to talk, to collaborate with the police and had nothing to do with it, or at least not all of it?' Frutos argued.

It was certainly a possibility they could not rule out, but for that they had to wait for the man who called himself Vasili to get back in touch with Frutos. And that had to be soon. The previous call could not be traced because no one in their right mind - not even Encinas and his CNI chief -

would have thought of tapping the superintendent's phone right there in the police station. It never crossed anyone's mind to organise an alert and recording system, waiting for the main suspect to contact the police.

After a couple of days, which seemed an eternity to Frutos and his team, Vasili called back. Frutos tried to calm him down and to boost his confidence and trust in the police. He promised him that his unsolicited confession and his cooperation with the police would be taken into account. But only in exchange for more information. Vasili was more afraid of Oleg's men than of the police and negotiated with Frutos a low-profile surrender, with police protection. They weren't prepared to come out of hiding and show themselves in Marbella, least of all to be seen in the company of the police. The superintendent guaranteed them maximum discretion and protection and explained the procedure to be followed.

Three days later two camouflaged police cars drove from Marbella to Rota. In one was Encinas and an assistant. In the other, a team from the Special Operations Group of the National Police (GEOS), armed and equipped, just in case things got nasty.

The plan was very simple: the rendezvous would be in a discreet location in town, on the outskirts, near a petrol station, where there wouldn't be too much traffic or prying eyes. They would greet Vasili and Grigori as if they were friends and each of them would get into one of the vehicles. They would not be handcuffed. It made no sense for them to try to escape when they had voluntarily given themselves up.

Later, when they arrived at the police station, they would enter through a side entrance, for authorised use only, and would be taken to a special area, where they would be permanently under surveillance and where there was no possibility of being discovered. The plan seemed safe and they readily accepted it.

As arranged, they met at the petrol station at the agreed time and after the sham greetings, each of them got into one of the two cars, guarded by two GEOS.

On the way back to Marbella the officers accompanying the Russians were chatty and friendly, showing respect and kindness. They offered them water and even some energy bars to kill their hunger. They didn't want to risk stopping in a public place to eat and, by shear sodding bad luck, meeting up with exactly the people they were trying to avoid.

Vasili and Grigori, meanwhile, kept silent, but both of them were wondering when the beatings would start. They could not yet fully comprehend the behaviour of the Spanish police.

The journey took just over two hours. The vehicles travelled along the motorway at break-neck speed and only slowed down as they entered the province of Malaga and snaked along the winding coastline to Marbella.

Once at the police station, they were taken to the holding room where the superintendent was waiting for them. He greeted them and told them that there were legal formalities to be carried out, i.e. they had to be read their rights and fingerprinted. After which, Frutos' first question took them by surprise:

'Have you eaten?'

Vasili and Grigori looked at each other as if they thought this was going to be some kind of macabre, sadistic joke. They both tentatively shook their heads.

'Would you like something to eat, a sandwich, perhaps?'

Grigori, who was really hungry, stepped forward.

'Whatever you have. Anything would do.'

Frutos gave one of his men some money and sent him to the sandwich machine. He also offered them each a large bottle of water, which they downed in a few gulps. Once their basic needs were taken care of, Frutos started to speak:

'Do you want a lawyer present? You have the right. You also have the right to say nothing.'

'Thank you, Superintendent. What we're going to tell you is the entire truth.'

'Alright. I'm listening.'

From that moment on, Vasili and Grigori were separated so that they could give their version of events and their stories could be compared. Who contacted them, where, how, what happened, how they were given the stolen car, the key, and so on. From time to time, while they were giving their statements, both Inspector Encinas and Frutos and others amongst those present interrupted the account to ask questions, many of which were simply to check if they were telling the truth.

Once they had finished their statements, Frutos brought them together again.

'Gentlemen, in view of your statements, you are under arrest as suspects in the robbery. Until you are presented to the judge, you will remain in these premises. Afterwards, if the judge orders you to be remanded in custody, we will request that you be placed in an isolation block. This is to ensure that you are protected from those you have been in contact with in connection with the robbery. Your alleged persecutors. Have you understood all that?'

'Yes.'

'As agreed, we will request that your cooperation and unsolicited surrender be taken into account. The fact that you both had jobs and had started a process of settling down should also be taken into consideration. For the time being, that is all I have to say. Now, get some rest.'

It was not the first time that Giorgi and Vasili had been in a prison or detention centre together, but it certainly seemed like a hotel compared to what they had known in the past. If it hadn't been for the girls they had left behind in Rota, they would almost have been happy to stay there.

The girls. That was the hardest part. It had taken a lot of courage for Vasili to own up to his girlfriend. Many times, while telling her what had happened, he had been unable to look her in the face. And when he did, he saw the tears running down her face and tissues littering the table in his flat. He had asked her there for the sake of privacy. There was no question of going to a café and causing a scene. And the truth is that Vasili was surprised by two things: first, that she agreed to go to his place on the grounds that what he had to tell her was very important and could not be done in a public place. And secondly, that as he went on with his story, his girl did not get up and leave. She stood there, crying, disappointed, disillusioned, disenchanted and heartbroken. But she stuck it out to the end. When Vasili finished, she looked him in the eye and asked:

'Why have you told me all this? You didn't have to. You could have kept me in the dark for the rest of my life and I would never have known. Why tell me?'

Vasili had asked himself that question too. He had had the same idea. And after a lot of thought, he had come to a realisation that explained everything.

'Because I love you and I don't want there to be any secrets between us. I am what I am. I've done what I've done. I can't change that. But you make me want to be a better person. I understand that I've let you down and that from now on you may not want to have anything to do with me. They're going to put me in prison. I don't know how long and it's possible that when I get out you won't be there. I can understand that. Or that they may be waiting for me to settle the score. I can't control all that. What I can do is tell you the truth about who I am and who I want to be.'

She had been listening to him in silence. A silence broken only by her sobs and the noise of her blowing her nose with tissues.

She stopped crying. She looked into his eyes and said nothing. Then she got up from her chair. Vasili thought it was to walk out of the house. He would never see her again. And that hurt him more than prison ever could and more than a bullet in the head or in the heart. Then she came up to him and kissed him, slipping her arms around his neck.

25.   Daniel in Monaco (2)

Edwin van Antwerp was an expert valuer, broker and dealer in art and antiques, operating both in Paris and Monte Carlo. A collector and connoisseur, he also worked on behalf of a certain David Orenstein, one of the patriarchs of a legendary and highly controversial dynasty of great collectors, dealers and traffickers, accused by several Jewish families of having enriched themselves through Nazi plunder.

Daniel thought it would be ironic and cruel if this Orenstein had anything to do with the theft, considering that it was the Nazis who first stole it from Bukowski's family.

It was rumoured that Orenstein's private collection amounted to a staggering ten thousand works of art by some of the greatest painters of all time: a score of Renoirs, a dozen Van Goghs, numerous Gauguins and Cézannes, several Grecos, a Botticelli, a Tintoretto, a Rembrandt, and so on. It would not be surprising if an officially uncatalogued Dürer had whetted his insatiable appetite. He was a shark, one of those "specimens" that debase the wonderful world of art.

Given his hunger for acquisition and his unfettered avarice Daniel had planned to use him as a means to an end, much like a bloodhound in search of the prey.

The next morning, Daniel woke up in his hotel suite. He had deliberately not set the alarm clock. He wasn't normally a heavy sleeper, but since he couldn't hear any noise and everything was dark, he looked at the clock and was amazed: he had slept for nine hours straight, which, for him, was unheard of. He felt an unusual burst of energy and attributed it to the long hours of sleep. He jumped out of bed and went to the living room. When he opened the door of his bedroom, he found that the lounge was suffused with a warm but blinding light. He covered his eyes with one hand as he turned back to go to the bathroom. In the shower he began to fully wake up. All he needed now, once he'd finished his ablutions, was a good cup of coffee for breakfast.

The hotel buffet offered all sorts of delicacies, including champagne for those who wanted it. *A little early*, thought Daniel, who was pretty conventional when it came to breakfast. Toast and jam, some fruit and a couple of white coffees were all he needed. After finishing, he looked at his watch, left the hotel and took a taxi. The address he gave the driver was the art gallery that Edwin van Antwerp owned in the principality.

Inside the gallery, he made a pretence of studying the paintings and sculptures that adorned the halls. He had been wandering around for a while and was appalled at the poor quality of the exhibits and the exorbitant prices - insultingly high for the calibre - when a gentleman approached him to ask if he could be of any assistance.

'I can't find what I'm looking for.'

'And what are you looking for, sir?'

'A sketch attributed to Dürer.'

The man froze, it was obvious he knew exactly what he was talking about.

'We have nothing by Dürer, sir.'

'Perhaps you might have something in the near future?'

'I doubt it, sir.'

'Would you be able to put me in touch with someone who might? My client is very interested in obtaining this particular artwork and would be willing to reward generously anyone who could help. For their trouble.'

'I understand, sir. I'll see what I can do to help you. Please wait a moment.'

And at a brisk pace he slipped through a doorway leading to the offices and his boss. That was exactly what Daniel had wanted.

After a couple of minutes, Daniel saw a tall, stocky, unfriendly-looking man coming towards him.

'Good morning,' he said. 'I'm Edwin...'

'I know who you are,' Daniel interrupted. 'What you don't know is who I am.'

The other man waited in silence for the mysterious gentleman, who had so boldly presented himself at his gallery, to disclose his identity.

'My name is Daniel. Daniel Olavarría. My client - an art-loving man - has delegated me a mission: to obtain **at any price**,' he stressed 'a self-portrait drawing attributed to Dürer. Wherever it is and whatever it costs. I thought that perhaps you could point me in the right direction.'

After the few moments it took him to recover from the shock of this proposition, the gallery owner managed to say:

'Please come with me to my office. We can talk more freely there.'

Before sitting down, Edwin van Antwerp asked him if he wanted something to drink and Daniel asked for some water. The lavish breakfast had made him thirsty.

'What makes you think I can solve your problem? You come here, to my gallery with no proper introduction and make veiled accusations?'

'Oh, no, please! I have been a little maladroit. Forgive me, I beg your pardon. I meant no disrespect. Quite the contrary. I know of your remarkable expertise and I thought that perhaps you might know something I don't. According to my information, the artwork

I am looking for is quite likely to have arrived in Monaco recently. And since it concerns an artist such as Dürer and an exceptional piece, I thought that you might...'

'I understand. I accept your apology.'

From that moment on, a sort of game of cat and mouse ensued between the two of them. A game in which Daniel would throw a ball to the cat so that the cat would pounce on it, at the same time as the cat had to give the impression that the ball was not his, nor did he know where it was, nor was he very interested in it. But there was one unquestionable truth: if Edwin van Antwerp was not interested in the matter, what were they doing talking about it in his office?

Daniel then added another turn of the screw.

'As I have already told you, my client is willing to be generous, not only to the current owner, but to anyone who might assist in successfully locating the picture.'

'Could you clarify the extent of your client's generosity?'

'10% of the value paid to the current owner.'

That certainly appealed to the avaricious side of Edwin van Antwerp, and his brain quickly set the calculator in motion. At lightning speed he began to plot a deal that would be very lucrative. He would contact the current owner, whom he knew personally and with whom he had excellent relations. His plan was to reach an agreement with the Qatari to raise the price as much as possible and share the profits.

'Are you authorised to sign a contract?'

'Of course,' replied Daniel.

'And how do I know you're not a policeman?'

'Because if I were, I would be out of my jurisdiction. And if not, you'd already be under arrest. Besides, you're only going to give me the name and address of the current owner and that doesn't commit you to anything. You don't have to worry.'

'I will have to make enquiries. Are you staying in the Principality?'

'At the Ambassador Imperator hotel.'

'I will get back to you as soon as possible.'

'Fine, until later, then. I'll wait to hear from you.'

'Yes, we'll speak soon.'

Daniel had a couple of days off, but first he had to make two calls. One to Bukowski, the other to Frutos.

26. Start of stage two - Vietnam

Once the first stage of the operation had been completed and the agent to take charge of the second stage had been chosen, two basic tasks had to be undertaken simultaneously.

One was to give the official order to start manufacturing the weapons, and the other was to prepare the ground at their destination: Vietnam. Ultimately, that was the purpose of the theft and subsequent sale: to obtain financing to manufacture an arsenal that would be delivered to a designated party in a friendly country like Vietnam.

As for the manufacture of the weaponry, it would naturally be entrusted to Krostec, the state-run enterprise that brought together all the manufacturers of all civilian and military equipment owned by the Russian state. Its headquarters was in Moscow, on the right bank of the Moskva River, at the point where the river meanders as it flows through the capital to which it gives its name.

Krostec combines around seven hundred enterprises within fourteen holding companies, eleven of which are active in the defence industry. Its subsidiaries are located in sixty regions of the Russian Federation and supply products to more than seventy countries. It is estimated to employ almost five hundred thousand people.

Igor Ruskin instructed Dimitri Kuznetsov to organise a meeting to formalise the operation, classified as 'TOP SECRET', with the following people:

Sergei Yakovlev (CEO of Krostec), the Minister of Trade and Industry of the Russian Federation and Chairman of the Board of Directors, the Undersecretary of Defence and the Minister of Finance.

While production began at the facility, preparations had to be made in

Vietnam.

To this end, the President of the Russian Federation called the Minister of Foreign Affairs, Aleksei Bogomolov to his office for a top-secret, late-night meeting with FSB chief Dimitri Kuznetsov. Igor was blunt:

'Minister, you must contact the embassy in Vietnam immediately to notify them of this operation.

I must stress,' he continued 'that this operation is of the utmost importance for the country and consists of delivering weapons to Vietnam, so that they can be handed over to the appropriate party. The ambassador must establish contact with the civilian and military authorities as necessary, with the aim of removing all obstacles and restrictions, both at customs and in any sectors affected by this large-scale operation. He will use whatever means are necessary to achieve this.

Have you got that?'

'Yes, President.'

'The weapons must arrive by sea to Hai Phong from our port in Magadan.'

'Understood, sir.'

'By the time the weapons arrive, all barriers must have been overcome or removed. Is that clear?'

'Yes, President.'

'If the ambassador needs extra funding, you will ensure it is provided.'

'Yes, sir. You can count on me.'

Aleksei Bogomolov realised, of course, that the president had not informed him what the weapons would be used for, what kind of weapons they were, or to whom they were to be delivered. And he deduced that none of this was an oversight. So it didn't even cross his mind to ask. Especially not with Dimitri present. It was clear that something big was brewing, but he couldn't believe it could be a war. Especially not with a friendly allied country. Maybe it was to prevent a foreign invasion? China? He didn't understand at all and didn't like any of the alternatives he could think of. So he would just do what the president had ordered him to do: contact the ambassador in Vietnam.

27.   Frutos: good news and bad news

In the last few days, Superintendent Frutos had been behaving in a way that was hindering the progress of the investigation, or so it seemed to Inspector Encinas.

Fermín Encinas who had been keeping a close eye on the superintendent for some time, had become convinced of this. It was of course also true that he had for some time had a secret source that was providing him with information unavailable to anyone else, and that gave him a great advantage over his colleague Eduardo, who had no idea what was going on.

Following the latest revelations and confessions, it had become urgent to pay another visit to the *Irina* nightclub in order to question the manager Oleg.

There was too much incriminating evidence pointing towards him.

Encinas, accompanied by three junior police officers, returned to the premises of the nightclub. The first thing that struck him was that there was no one on the door. When they came before, they had been greeted by a thug of a man with no neck. In fact, there was nobody there at all and the place seemed to be closed. He thought that maybe it was too early in the day and that they would open later. He pulled on the door anyway and was surprised to find that it was open.

Inside, a heavy silence prevailed, intermingled with the smell of tobacco. They entered very cautiously; in case it was a trap. Encinas reached down to his belt, undid the holster and rested his hand on his service weapon, a Heckler & Koch USP. A couple of the other officers with him followed suit, although none of them drew their pistols. They heard sounds coming from what appeared to be the kitchen. With the utmost care and attention, they fanned out and headed in that direction.

As they drew nearer, the clatter of dishes and voices grew louder. Step by step, they approached the hinged doors that led into the kitchen. Very slowly Encinas pushed one of the doors until he managed to open it without the people inside hearing anything. Suddenly, one of them saw them at the door and shouted something in a language the officers couldn't understand. Everyone there immediately became alarmed and several of them grabbed huge knives and advanced towards them in a most unfriendly manner. It was at that moment that Encinas drew his weapon with his right hand, while with his left hand he flashed his badge and shouted:

'Freeze, police! Drop the knives and get down on the ground! NOW!'

The men had stopped dead in their tracks and didn't seem to understand. They had desisted from attacking them at the sight of the guns and the badge but were unsure what to do next. Although they didn't understand what the police were shouting, they had a pretty clear idea.

Encinas realised that they didn't speak Spanish, and while still pointing his gun at them, he put his badge away and signalled with his left hand that they should lie down on the ground and drop the knives.

Once he had control of the situation, he ordered the kitchen staff to be handcuffed and called for a police van to take them to the station.

Before leaving the premises, Encinas looked around to see if he could find the manager or a waitress. He arrived at what looked like Oleg's office and rummaged through his papers. There was nothing of any use, nothing interesting, just invoices from suppliers and employee pay slips in folders neatly arranged on a bookcase on the wall. The place was empty.

When the kitchen staff arrived at the police station, they were put in the cells and as there was no one who could understand them, an interpreter was called to assist. The thought occurred to Encinas that she was called so often that it would be better to put her on the payroll.

One by one they passed through the interrogation room, but none of them opened their mouths. The interpreter translated the questions and answers, but the constant theme was that they didn't know anything. Apparently, they had been hired by a temporary employment agency to clean the kitchen and it was the first time they had been there. No one knew who Oleg was or where he or the waitresses were. They had vanished into thin air.

In the end, Encinas did not press charges against any of them on the basis that all they had done was try to defend themselves against intruders and that as soon as the police identified themselves, they had backed down and offered no resistance. That meant less paperwork. In any case, they were asked to voluntarily leave their contact details, address, telephone number, name, etc. None of them accepted the kind invitation.

Encinas knocked on the superintendent's door:

'Excuse me, sir.'

'Come in, Encinas. What have you got for me?'

'Nothing, sir.'

'Nothing?'

'Absolutely nothing. They're gone, sir. They've disappeared. It's as if they guessed we were coming back. The place is empty. We've only arrested some employees who were cleaning the kitchen and who have been hired by a temporary employment agency. They don't know anything. Conveniently, they don't even speak Spanish.'

Frutos reacted in a way that Encinas found very strange: he took a deep breath, as if he were relieved. It was difficult to explain what on earth was going on in his chief's head.

The departure indicated that they had had him in their grasp and that he had escaped them, probably for good. It was a serious setback, and yet Frutos didn't seem to care. Encinas took careful note but refrained from making any comment.

'That's fine, Encinas. We should follow up on the domestic staff of the victim of the robbery. I'm convinced there's an accomplice.'

'We'll question them again. This time we'll put more pressure on them.'

'All right. Keep me informed.'

'Of course, sir. Anything else?'

'No, that's all. Thank you, Encinas.'

As soon as the inspector left his office, his mobile phone rang. It was a very long, unfamiliar number, from outside the country. He was surprised that a stranger had got hold of his number. He answered the call.

'Yes?'

'Frutos. It's Daniel.'

'Jesus, mate! Where are you calling from? The number's bloody huge.'

'Yeah, I know. Listen, I've got something for you. But I need you to help me.'

'Fire away.'

'I think I'm about to find out who the buyer of the picture stolen from Bukowski's house was.'

'You're kidding! How did you manage that?'

'To be honest, I was lucky. I baited the hook to see if I'd catch something, though I didn't have much faith in it, and I got a surprise. I didn't expect it to be so stupidly simple.'

'And what do you need me for?'

'I have a plan to get the picture back. Free of charge. No ransom. I'll even give you the right to brag about it publicly. I'm only interested in my client, he's the one I'm contracted to. But I need your cooperation.'

'You can count on me. What do you need?'

'I need you to pull strings with Interpol.'

'What for?'

'We're probably going to bust an art trafficker and we'll need to arrest him on the spot. I presume Interpol can do that, can't they?'

'Jesus, Daniel, you're asking a hell of a lot. That's way beyond my jurisdiction. I'm sorry, I can't do that.'

Daniel was infuriated by the response. Frutos had not even said he would try but he couldn't promise anything. He had simply said "no". It left him speechless for a few moments, the time it took for the blow to sink in.

'Daniel?'

'Yes, I'm here. Well then, in that case, that's all. Thanks.'

And he hung up without waiting for Frutos to say goodbye.

Daniel couldn't accept that answer and remembered the strange offer Bukowski had made him: that he could turn to him for help, that he had contacts everywhere, even in hell.

Encinas hadn't told Frutos everything. No one else had been at the premises, it was true. That's why he was surprised that Frutos didn't tell him to find Oleg's home address and have him brought into the station. And, while he was at it, bring in the waitress, too.

But the fact that Frutos did not order him to do so did not mean that he couldn't act on his own initiative. So, when he got home in the evening, he again used the communication system with his secret informant.

I have to contact the waitress at the club, Marina. Very important.

Just as he was about to save it as a draft, he noticed a coincidence: his secret informant signed off as "M", although the email said "Tatiana".

28.   Oleg travels to Moscow

The party in honour of Oleg at his boss Ivan's palatial mansion was one of the most talked-about events in Marbella in recent years.

For the press, guests and onlookers, it was simply a party. One more party organised by the company *Destellos Marbella* in which the Russian and Spanish people were united in a friendly, sincere and beneficial symbiosis.

About five hundred guests attended, dressed for the occasion in their best attire. There were renowned businessmen from the property sector together with sporting personalities, the press, bankers, millionaires, *bon vivants*, families of noble lineage, peers, distinguished members of a European royal household and the odd nouveau riche. Anyone who was anyone was there and if they weren't, they were as good as dead socially speaking.

The party was a great success. The company that organised it didn't miss a single detail. At the entrance, the ladies were presented with fresh flowers and the gentlemen with miniatures of Gran Reserva wine.

Between the guests, their chauffeurs and the catering staff, there were times when it was difficult to move around the enormous gardens of the mansion. The garden lights provided a warmth and intimacy to the tables that were spread throughout the grounds, while a legion of waiters served champagne and hors d'oeuvres of every description on vast trays that emanated non-stop from the kitchen. In one corner of the huge garden a bar was set up, which was permanently manned by four bartenders serving the thirsty guests, some of whom were drinking like sponges. Bottles of the best vodka disappeared like water. Champagne had to be chilled by artificial means because the bottles were shifting so fast. Without any doubt, the tax the villa paid for rubbish collection was worth every penny that night.

The hors d'oeuvres were a fusion of the most refined Russian tradition with the most delectable Spanish tapas. The desserts were the same, a skilful blend of both cuisines.

Even the staff who inevitably accompany so many prominent figures were catered for. They stayed at the entrance to the estate, many of them with their cars, chatting amongst themselves and food and drink were brought to them there. This was greatly appreciated, as they were not always so well looked after. The catering manager even paid them a quick visit to check if everything was to their liking and if they needed anything else.

It was to be expected that at some point the Russian contingent would feel the need to indulge in a spot of karaoke, so, much to the delight of all those present, a stage had been constructed expressly for this purpose.

Before any of the participants, under the obvious influence of excessive alcohol, could take the microphone, Ivan himself stepped forward and addressed those present. Realising that most of them were either fluent in Spanish or at least understood it, he spoke to them in that language.

> 'Good evening, everyone. First of all, I wanted to thank you all for coming. I am honoured and very happy to be able to receive you in my house and delighted that you have accepted the invitation.'

There was a round of applause to thank to the host, after which he continued.

> 'I hope you're all having a good time and that you continue to enjoy the rest of the evening. I can only hope you don't go so far as to drink the water out of the flower vases.'

Widespread laughter at Ivan's mastery of the language.

'I won't ramble on any more and bore you all to tears. From now on, my friends, just keep on enjoying yourselves.'

The last remaining guests left the party almost at dawn. Throughout the night the catering staff had been collecting dozens of bags of rubbish in order to get a head start on the enormous amount of work they would have to do when it was over. That way they gained several hours of sleep.

When everything was cleared away, there was no trace of the party left, except for a few cigarette butts and some paper napkins on the lawn. But that would be taken care of by those responsible for its upkeep.

The party organiser sought out Ivan to ask if everything had been satisfactory and to say goodbye, speaking to her client in Russian.

'I congratulate you. It has been quite magnificent. I know who to come to for future events.'

'Thank you, Mr Orlov. I am very grateful for your kind words. We will be happy to be of service any time you need us.'

The only two left behind were Ivan and Oleg. When he too departed, Oleg would go straight to the airport and take the private jet to Moscow. His lover, Marina Smolensk, the waitress at the club, would stay in Marbella. It made no sense for her to be in Moscow while Oleg travelled the length and breadth of Asia by plane and boat.

His orders were to travel to the Russian capital to report to the president and Kuztnesov. Once there, he was to check and test the quality of the weaponry being manufactured and, once it was approved, head for the port of Magadan, in the easternmost part of Russia, on the Sea of Okhotsk. From there they would head for Hai Phong in Vietnam using a Russian freighter to conceal the cargo.

The port of Magadan was being used for logistical reasons. The range of the largest Russian military transport aircraft was not sufficient to reach Hai Phong directly and even if it had been capable of it, it would not be able to land there because the runway was too short. Therefore, the cargo had to be flown to Magadan, but with a stopover in Novosibirsk. A nightmare of a journey.

29.   Daniel travels to Qatar

Daniel was very surprised at the result of his enquiries. It was true that he was of the opinion that the unsavoury Edwin van Antwerp behaved much like an arachnid. He was the kind of man who spun a spider's web wherever he went, and as soon as he detected vibrations, he would rush over to find out what was going on. Once there, he would decide whether to gobble up the intruder or use him as bait for other, more succulent prey.

Daniel wanted to contact him because he was sure he could provide him with some kind of valuable information about the Dürer. Not free, of course, but something useful he could work with. As he was sure he had heard about the picture, he didn't beat about the bush and fired a volley hoping to get something in return, but the spider's riposte came as a shock.

After a couple of days, he received a call at his hotel. It wasn't the spider; it was some trusted employee and all the voice said was:

'Mahfuz Amirmoez. Doha,' and he hung up.

It was then that Daniel devised a plan, but he needed the help of his friend Frutos. He needed support.

After talking to the superintendent and not getting his cooperation, the only thing he could do was report back to his client.

'Mr Bukowski.'

'Hello, Daniel, my friend, how's it going?'

'I have good news, although there are still a lot of loose ends to tie up and a lot of things that could go wrong. I don't want to get your hopes up only to have them dashed. I am very conscious that "it's not over till the fat lady sings" and we should not "count our chickens before they hatch".

Bukowski was amused by Daniel's pearls of wisdom, but he understood what he was getting at. He couldn't help but feel much more encouraged, though. He was certainly closer to recovering the artwork now than he had been the day after it had been stolen.

'I also have some bad news,' Daniel continued.

'Go on.'

'Well, you see, I have information that places the picture with a certain amount of plausibility in Doha, the capital of Qatar.'

'Good.'

'Yes, but the problem is that I've asked Chief Superintendent Frutos in Marbella, who is a friend of mine, for help, and he's left me in the lurch. And without legal cover, I don't know what use it would be for me to go there. I can't just go to the man I believe to be the buyer and steal the painting from him. I have to have support from the authorities to back me up.'

'I understand and I completely agree with you. Stay in Monaco for the time it takes me to sort this out. Enjoy the sights, visit the casino and try your luck. In short, carpe diem, my friend Daniel, carpe diem. I'll call you back as soon as I've resolved your little problem.'

He took advantage of his free time and followed his client's advice. He would have preferred to enjoy the luxury with a female companion, such as his fiancée or who knows, his wife, but that was not the case. He could also hire someone, but that was too artificial.

In extremely affluent environments such as Monaco, there was an abundance of so-called "seagulls", a type of more or less sophisticated woman, who moves from one part of the coast to another in search of a fish to put in her mouth, one with a well-stocked wallet, without too many scruples, and, essentially, who will maintain her high standard of living in exchange for company, good conversation in several languages, excellent taste, and sex.

But what Daniel lacked most was a stable relationship. He certainly had plenty of opportunities to overcome his loneliness with sex, but he quickly realised that this was not what he needed.

After a couple of days of alcohol, casino and hangovers, he received the promised phone call from Bukowski.

'Daniel, my friend, where would you like me to start?'

'Let's hear the good news first.'

'I have arranged with my contact at Interpol to place an agent of sufficient authority at your service and to accompany you to Qatar. Once there, the two of you will decide what action to take.'

'Mr Bukowski, do you really have contacts with Interpol?'

'And with others that you couldn't begin to imagine.'

'You never cease to amaze me. So, I can leave for Doha?'

'Whenever you're ready. I'll give you the name of the agent you are to meet up with there. By the way, since you're staying in Doha, I strongly recommend that you stay at the most exclusive hotel in the capital. The Majestic.'

'Mr Bukowski. Don't tell me that...'

'Haha, yes. I'm afraid so, my dear friend.'

'My goodness. I seem to be doing a tour of your establishments. I hope you're not going to ask me to give you a report on each one later.'

'Carpe diem, Daniel, my friend. And no, don't worry, I already have other people to do that for me.'

'Thank you, but there is one thing.'

'Yes.'

'It's going to be two rooms and not one.'

'And where's the problem in that? Don't worry about such trifles.'

'Great. Once again, thank you very much. I'll keep you up to date.'

'Please rely on my jet to fly you to Doha. The crew is there in Monaco awaiting your orders. In fact, I'm surprised you haven't bumped into each other at the hotel.'

'That's because it's so damn big.'

'Haha, yes. That's probably why. Now I'll call the captain and tell him to put himself at your disposal.'

'Thanks very much, sir.'

'Thank you. Have a good trip.'

Daniel needed to contact a colleague in the Qatari emirate. He wanted to inform him of his intentions and also to talk to him about Mahfuz Amirmoez, the alleged trafficker and buyer of the stolen picture.

His friend was a member of ARCA, the Association for Research into Crimes against Art, an organisation whose interventions had prevented the disappearance of countless pieces of antiquity from all over the Middle East. Such crimes were the result of the limitless greed of those who did not hesitate to plunder any national treasure and of the ignorance of those for whom these pieces of art simply represented food for their family for a week. They were not always in time to rescue all works of art before they were introduced into the black market, but they were happy enough to save a few dozen each year. Trying to save everything was impossible, and many of the governments involved just weren't interested.

Looking up his number on his mobile, he sent his friend a WhatsApp to tell him that he would soon be arriving in Doha in search of a stolen picture and that he needed to see him. He told him that he would be staying at the Majestic Hotel, where they would meet and that he should wait to hear from him. After a few minutes his friend replied with two emojis; a smiley face and a thumbs-up.

He then contacted the person Bukowski had arranged for him to meet, to give him the name of the hotel where he would be staying and to set up a meeting in the hotel.

A little later, he received a call from the captain of the private jet. Before they could leave, he needed a day to prepare the plane, check the mechanics, fill the tanks, and complete the paperwork and formalities for the trip to Doha.

Everything was arranged and in order. He hoped that everything would go as anticipated. All that remained was to take off and reach his destination.

30.   A party in Hanoi

Immediately after Igor Ruskin had closed the meeting in his office and given the appropriate orders, Russia's foreign minister Aleksei Bogomolov called the Russian ambassador in Vietnam on a secure line. He didn't know what time it would be there, but he didn't care. The matter was top priority.

It was clear from the ambassador's voice that he had got him out of bed. That was probably why he used a tone that forced the diplomat to wake up with a start and pay close attention to what his immediate superior was telling him. He faithfully relayed the president's orders and made it clear to his ambassador that these instructions came from the top. His mission, he stressed, was to do ***whatever was necessary*** to ensure that the shipment would not encounter the slightest obstacle, of any kind, in any civilian or military jurisdiction in the country. And that any problems would have to be resolved immediately.

The ambassador, who began in a daze as he answered the phone because he had been called in the middle of the night, ended up with his eyes wide open and his heart racing, wondering what kind of scheme the Kremlin had devised to warrant such an operation.

After receiving his boss's instructions, and since going back to bed did not seem a very wise option under the circumstances, he decided to wake up all the personnel working for the embassy and even the Under Secretary of State. He called his butler, who had also been woken up by the telephone, and while he showered, ordered him to call the next in line, who would then call their subordinates. He looked at the clock and it was three o'clock in the morning. The order was to meet at the embassy at four o'clock.

When the ambassador arrived at the official residence most of his staff were waiting for him, although some from the lower ranks had been delayed. Taxis were not easy to find at that hour and those levels did not have official cars. Nevertheless, when he saw that the main members of his team were present, he began the meeting.

With the same firmness and in a tone very similar to that which the minister had used with him, he conveyed to them the orders *that came from the highest echelons*, as well as the directive that whatever had to be done, had to be done NOW!

Sleepy faces instantly gave way to faces that oscillated from astonishment to deep concern. They were being asked to do whatever was necessary to make an arms shipment that was due to arrive in the country, become completely invisible. Some thought, without mentioning it aloud, of the illusionist David Copperfield, but the difference was that he was not going to be sent to Siberia if the magic trick didn't work.

Among those present - most trying to wake up, others trying to cope with the shock of the news - one timidly raised his hand.

'Yes, do you have a question?' the ambassador asked.

'No, sir. I wanted to make a suggestion.'

'Someone who is capable of thinking at this hour? Go ahead, young man. Astound us.'

'Well, you see, sir, I thought maybe we could have a party, here at the embassy.'

His colleagues looked at him in terror, thinking he had gone mad or was under the influence of some psychotropic drug.

'Before or after they shoot us all?'

There were a few sniggers.

'No, sir. You see, the idea is to summon to the embassy all the important personalities, both civilian and military, who might be involved in the procedure for the entry of the goods.'

The young man paused for a few seconds to see what reaction the first part of his proposal had elicited.

'Please continue.'

'The reason for the party doesn't matter. The important thing is that everyone is here. Once the party starts, they would all be drugged, although they would not lose consciousness. They would simply no longer be in control of their behaviour.'

'Carry on.'

'Right, well then, we would need to hire some local prostitutes. Their job would be to take everyone to the bedrooms, which would be set up in advance to record everything that took place there.'

He fell silent again to see if anyone would burst out laughing or if the ambassador would announce his next posting to the North Pole. Seeing that neither was happening, he finished off his plan.

'That way we could put pressure on them under threat of making public images that would end their careers, their social standing, their financial rackets and probably also their marriages.'

A heavy silence filled the room, which was beginning to show the effects of the presence of so many people in a confined space and in a climate with an average humidity of 80%. They all turned their heads to watch the ambassador's reaction.

'Anyone got a better idea?'

The silence confirmed the plausibility of the brave young man's words.

Then the ambassador, in a much friendlier manner, looked at them all, moving his head from side to side, very slowly, and fixing his gaze on each and every one of them. He uttered a single sentence:

'Right, do it. Now!'

31.   Daniel recovers the picture

Daniel was getting a taste for travelling by private jet, staying in deluxe hotels, being chauffeur-driven and all this for free. He was like those actors and actresses who, at some Hollywood gala, show off their jewellery, watches and glamorous outfits, none of which they actually own. They are simply being used as models in a gigantic shop window and, on top of that, they profit from it, either by being able to attend certain events for free or even by receiving money. Well, he felt somewhat like that.

This particular job had many unusual features. He was used to travelling the world, that was not new to him, but he had never done so in so much style. Nor had he ever been under such pressure to retrieve a work of art as quickly as possible. However, on this occasion, the client had warned him of his advancing age and that he might not have sufficient time left to recover the Dürer sketch, which added a further degree of urgency to the matter. Furthermore, it was not often that there was murder involved in addition to the theft. Although, in truth, he never imagined that he would later have so much luck in his efforts to recover it. He had thought at first that he would have to deal with the Russian mafia or worse, and it turned out that a little prodding of the Belgian was all it needed.

After a five-hour flight, he landed at Doha International Airport. He then went through the administrative and customs formalities, and once again found that Bukowski had arranged for a limousine, of the region's finest style, to transport himself and the crew. It made sense, as they were all staying at the same hotel.

Upon arrival at the hotel, three or four attendants, dressed in immaculate uniforms, hurried to the boot of the limousine to retrieve the guests' luggage. All the suitcases were loaded onto a trolley for transport and they followed the five passengers to Reception.

The luxurious building was situated on the edge of the Persian Gulf and its more than twenty brightly lit floors shone out over the water as if it were a lighthouse, creating sinuous shapes that continually morphed with the rhythm of the waves.

After checking in, Daniel asked for the person Aaron had arranged for him to meet, and the concierge told him she had already arrived.

They dispersed to their various bedrooms accompanied by two attendants who transferred their suitcases to their rooms.

After taking possession of his room, Daniel unpacked his suitcase and took a refreshing shower. Straight after, he called his friend, Mohamed Alfarsi, to whom he had already announced his arrival via WhatsApp. They arranged to meet in the bar of the hotel in fifteen minutes.

He then called the room of his Interpol contact. As they did not know each other, Daniel proposed that he stop by the room and they go down to the bar together so that the three of them could meet up.

He rapped on the door of the room with his knuckles and when it opened he met Carmen, the Interpol commander who was going to be supporting Daniel in this operation.

She was a little shorter than Daniel, a brunette with a slim figure, dressed in a conservative outfit. Carmen's job, in most cases, required her to wear attire that didn't draw attention to herself, and for this particular one, and because it was a Muslim country, it seemed the most appropriate thing to do.

Daniel reckoned she must be in her late forties and still looking good for her age.

'Good evening, I'm Commander Riviera,' she said as she opened the door, shaking his hand firmly.

'Pleased to meet you. I'm Daniel Olavarría, but please call me Daniel. I've set up a meeting with a friend from here who is with the ARCA association to give us an update on the individual we need to visit. We're meeting downstairs in the bar.'

'That's great. Let's go, then. And please, call me Carmen.'

They looked for a table a little out of the way, discreet, but at the same time allowing Daniel to keep an eye out for when his friend Mohamed arrived. While they waited for him, they ordered two orange juices. Alcohol was available to guests, but when it came to work - and this meeting was - neither Daniel nor Carmen felt tempted. Across the room, Daniel spotted some of the aircrew and raised a hand to them. Bukowski had given him some background information on her. She had never married. She had put work before family. In that sense, they were quite alike. Carmen Riviera de las Torras y Grande Benjumea - that was the commander's full name - belonged to a family of noble descent, with a title thrown in for good measure. Her family and her social status provided her with an excellent education in the most prestigious schools in various European countries (Switzerland, UK...). She also studied art at the Sorbonne, Bologna, Holland and in the UK. She was fluent in English, French, German, Italian and Arabic, one of the main reasons why she was chosen for this operation. She was reportedly studying Russian. Without a doubt, the commander's professional profile was impressive.

As Mohamed was delayed for a while, Carmen and Daniel took the opportunity to exchange a few professional confidences. He updated her on the details of the robbery and she expressed great interest in Daniel's methods. Finally, Mohamed came up to them and apologised for the delay. He had wanted to finish verifying some of the info before passing it on to his friends.

After a warm embrace, Daniel introduced the two of them, and then they moved on to the business that had brought them together.

Mohamed described the current owner, Mahfuz Amirmoez, as a lavish spender who was uncultured and unscrupulous when it came to buying works of art. He cared nothing about the provenance of the pieces. He belonged to that class of people who, living in a social and economic bubble, believe they are invulnerable.

The commander pointed out that Interpol had long suspected that he might be laundering money, although it was not yet known exactly from whom.

Daniel mentioned that this Mahfuz had already been alerted to his presence, because it was likely that the infamous Edwin van Antwerp had called him from Monaco. He suspected, although he had no proof, that this same Edwin had arranged a deal with Mahfuz, in order to get as much money out of them as possible and split the profits. Therefore, he could not present himself to the owner as having been recommended by van Antwerp. So he asked how they could approach the individual without arousing suspicion, and Mohamed suggested the simplest method: to ask for his advice on the purchase of a piece of art. For a man who is totally ignorant about art, nothing satisfies the ego more than to be taken for an expert. The important thing was that he should receive them in his palace. And if it was true that the Belgian had come to an agreement with him, the chances were that he would offer it to them at his own volition, at an exorbitant price. Once inside, events would unfold according to their natural course.

'And when do you reckon he'll be able to see us?' Daniel asked.

'I'll call him today and propose a meeting at his palace. I will tell him the story we have just agreed. The three of us will go, of course. Although he and I are not close friends, we know each other because we move in the same art scene that lies within that fine line between trading and trafficking. I'm sure that as soon as I tell him I have a buyer with no spending limit, his greed will get the better of him.'

'D'you think we might be able to get an appointment for tomorrow?'

'It's quite likely. Especially if it's true that he's already been tipped off that you're coming. I'll call you later to confirm.'

Once they were up to speed on all elements of the case, the rest of the time was spent enjoying excellent cocktails - except for Mohamed - and an interesting, enlightening and entertaining discussion of fine art, art theft and plundering.

After a while Mohamed excused himself and said he had some things to do, including calling the supposed relative of the emir.

Later, while Daniel was relaxing in his room, his mobile rang. As Mohamed had predicted, the appointment would be the next day. Daniel then called Bukowski to let him know.

'What time do you need the driver, Daniel?'

'The appointment's at noon.'

'Right. Half an hour before, the car will be at the gate waiting for you. I'll take care of it.'

'Thank you once again.'

'Good luck. And don't forget, I'm willing to pay a ransom if it's necessary.'

'Don't worry, sir. I'm confident that won't be necessary.'

It was still early. Daniel was feeling hungry and then an idea occurred to him. He called through to Carmen's room.

'I hope I'm not disturbing you.'

'Not at all. What can I do for you?'

'My friend just called me. The appointment's tomorrow at noon. Half an hour before, the driver will be waiting at the gate to take the three of us to Mahfuz's palace.'

'OK. Fine. Anything else?'

'Yes, there is. The truth is I'm a bit hungry and I hate eating alone. I was wondering if you'd like to grab a bite to eat.'

'Yeah, sure. Great.'

'Do you generally like Arabic food or do you prefer something more Western?'

'Wherever you normally eat, it's up to you. I'm inclined to go local.'

'That's great. Shall we meet in the lobby in, say, 15 minutes?

'Done.'

***

The vehicle passed through the entrance of Mahfuz's immense estate at the appointed time. Inside sat Carmen and Daniel, as the purported buyers of art for a client with no spending limit, and Mohamed, as the intermediary in the ostensible business deal. The entrance drive was in itself a display of arrogance and vanity. If the intention was to overwhelm the visitor, it certainly succeeded, and the sensation reached new heights when the vehicle stopped in front of the main entrance of this palace of cyclopean dimensions.

Carmen had wisely chosen a very formal outfit for the occasion and had covered her head with a scarf, simulating the *Shayla* worn by some Arab women. Her regulation pistol and Interpol badge were in her handbag.

Walking up the grand staircase to the entrance of the palace, one had the impression of being received by a representative of some European monarchy. And indeed, this was exactly the result that was intended.

A servant led them through endless corridors with spotless, shining floors. The walls were filled with paintings of every different style, school and taste, with no thought having been given to their arrangement other than to hang them in the order in which they were acquired, thus lowering art to its lowest possible status, as mere decoration.

> 'It's a pleasure to receive you in my humble abode,' the host said,
> in a supreme effort to appear to be what he clearly was not.
> 'Thank you for seeing us at such short notice.'
> 'Please, do sit down.'

Then he clapped his hands and four servants appeared as if by magic, each carrying a huge, silver-embossed tray offering various kinds of tea, as well as fruit, dates, sweets and desserts. Arab hospitality obliged, and the rules of good conduct required, that a cup of tea should never be refused. That would be considered an insult. One of the servants was in charge of attending to his master and another did the same for the guests, who, despite the hour, accepted the tea and the occasional item of confectionery.

Once the proper protocol had been respected, they went on to discuss the reason for their presence there.

The conversation began by raising the possibility of acquiring some of the works of art in which they were theoretically interested. As is well known, in any negotiation with an Arab, one must be patient and, above all, never give the impression of being in a hurry. And even more so when what is on the table is of enormous cultural value and, in economic terms, worth tens of millions.

The gentleman began to point out all the pictures he had on display on the walls, showing them around as if his palace were a gallery. Daniel, Carmen and Mohamed all had to suppress certain comments and facial expressions when faced with the eyesores that this wealthy idiot was so proudly pointing out.

Then they came across a sketch, a self-portrait by Dürer. Daniel's pulse began to race and he thought that his heartbeat must surely be audible to everyone. But he managed to conceal his feelings and pass by as if the drawing was worthless. And that was what aroused the owner's conceit: that the picture, which had cost him so much money, was not being sufficiently appreciated. Moreover, his Belgian friend had told him that the buyer was very interested in this particular piece. So, when they had passed the picture, Mahfuz retraced his steps and remarked:

'This is my latest acquisition, what do you think?'

Daniel, who now had his attitude and his response under control, approached the painting, feigning interest prompted by the host. After a few seconds he surprised everyone:

'I hope you didn't spend too much. It's a fake.'

Mahfuz gave him a furious look and tried to impress him.

'I paid a lot of money for it, my good fellow. And two independent experts have vouched for its authenticity.'

'Did you buy it from Ivan Orlov?'

Mahfuz stood looking shocked, without saying a word.

'That's typical of him. I know him very well. He usually sends two specialists in order to give the impression that they're independent.

But the truth is that they've both been bribed beforehand. It's a fake. In fact, if you let me take a look, I can confirm it.'

Although visibly shaken and unnerved, the man immediately proceeded to take down the painting and remove the frame - which, by the way, was hideous, Carmen thought - and allow his guests to analyse it. He had no choice but to swallow the insult.

Daniel had specific instructions from Bukowski to identify the painting's authenticity. Carmen knew this because they had discussed it the day before in the hotel bar. They were to scrutinise the eyes of the self-portrait with a high magnifying glass and discover a series of specific dates and numbers that would only mean something to someone who knew the work and its author.

They both analysed the work with care and painstaking attention to detail. Daniel was convinced that his heart was going to burst out of his chest. He found it increasingly hard to breathe.

'I'm sorry, Mr Mahfuz. In my opinion, it's a fake,' Daniel concluded.

'I agree,' said Carmen, who had chosen to remain in the background. She was, after all, in a traditional Muslim country where women's behaviour is very restricted, especially commenting on a matter normally dealt with by men.

Mahfuz's face was a poem. He was sweating profusely and seemed on the verge of losing his senses.

'It can't be. It can't be,' he repeated like a mantra over and over again.

He looked incredulously at his guests and wondered what they were up to. A couple who had been recommended by his good friend Edwin van Antwerp and who, according to him, were prepared to pay anything for this Dürer portrait. It was clear, he thought, that they were trying to devalue the work. He could see it all, now.

'I'm sorry, but this is more than I'm willing to put up with. It is one thing to open a negotiation and another to try what you are attempting to do.'

At that point, Carmen took her Interpol commander's badge out of her bag and, while showing it to him and identifying herself, ordered him to sit down:

'Take a seat, Mr Amirmoez, and don't do anything stupid.'

Once again, he was taken by surprise and, even worse, this time a woman was giving him orders in his own house.

'I am going to explain the situation to you. This picture you possess is not only a stolen artwork, for which, for a start, you will have to account to Interpol because I'm going to accuse you of trafficking in works of art. In addition, you are also an accomplice in the murder of two people connected with the theft in Marbella in Spain. One way and another, you can't possibly get less than thirty years in prison. In Spain, of course, which is where the events took place.'

'I don't know what you are talking about, madam, and please don't speak to me in that tone. You are in my house and what's more, you are a wo...'

Then, before he could finish his sentence and utter the fateful word "woman" to insult her, Commander Riviera interrupted him and addressed him in Arabic. Daniel didn't understand what she said, but from the looks on the faces of both Amirmoez and Mohamed, it was clear that it wasn't very friendly. However, she managed to get him to respect her and address her in a different, more deferential tone.

'I don't know what murders you're talking about. This has nothing to do with me. I'm just a businessman who likes art...'

'You are a trafficker in works of art, which is not the same thing. On the walls of your house I have detected more than half a dozen items that have been stolen from museums and private collections. And I'm sure that when they finish their work, the team of experts that's on its way here will strip the palace bare.'

The man was confused and looked quite pale. He was agitated and breathing heavily. He looked like he was about to have a seizure.

'For the time being, I am requisitioning this artwork attributed to Dürer on behalf of Interpol and I'm taking it with me right now. Please sign this document acknowledging this act of voluntary surrender,' she said, handing over the document she had already prepared on Interpol's official letterhead.

Amirmoez was living a nightmare and he sensed that it was not going to end there. Sure enough, suddenly they heard the footsteps of a large group of people bursting into his palace and heading towards them. There was a dozen of them, including members of the Doha police force and others from Interpol. At the head of the group was a colonel.

'Mr Mahfuz Amirmoez, you are under arrest for trafficking and smuggling works of art,' he said as he slapped a pair of handcuffs on him.

32.   Oleg travels to Vietnam

The farewell party that Ivan threw in Oleg's honour dominated most of that week's gossip magazines.

After the party Oleg and his girlfriend Marina went straight to the airport. He boarded his private jet to Moscow and Marina returned home.

Oleg had a busy few weeks ahead of him, between planes, the ship, paperwork and the delivery of the cargo to its destination. What worried him most was specifically the destination. The success of the whole operation lay in the fact that when it arrived, the entire Vietnamese civilian and military apparatus would have been deactivated to eliminate a diplomatic problem. Furthermore, it was an operation in which he had not been involved and he did not like to trust strangers that he knew nothing about.

After a seven-hour flight, Oleg landed in Moscow. The next step was to meet President Ruskin. The aim was to present himself to the president to introduce himself in person and get his approval, although the latter was a mere formality. Recommended by the great Ivan, and with so little time to find a possible replacement, any other alternative was virtually unthinkable.

Once that meeting was over, Oleg and Dmitry Kuznetsov visited the facilities of the Rosoboronexport and Kalashnikov Consortium where the weapons were manufactured. There they were received by the senior management of the complex and together they reviewed the military equipment. Oleg made a thorough analysis of the rifles and even tested some of them on the shooting range at the facility. He checked the smoothness of the mechanisms, whether the front and rear sights were properly calibrated, whether the quality of the firearms corresponded to what they were supposed to be, whether they jammed when firing, etc. After doing a spot check, he considered that he could give the go-ahead. The boxes were then sealed, labelled and loaded onto army trucks for transport to Moscow Domodedovo International Airport. The next day, his superior handed him the false documentation that he was to show to the cargo ship's captain and present on his arrival in Hai Phong.

Once in the restricted military area of the airport, the consignment was loaded onto a Russian cargo plane, the Antonov An-225, bound for Magadan.

The first leg of the journey took him from Moscow to Novosibirsk. Almost four hours in a godforsaken cargo plane. Nothing comparable to the comforts of the private jet with its stewardesses and readily available luxuries.

Arriving in Novosibirsk, he and the crew took a break for a bite to eat. There was still another five and a half hours of flying to go, not to mention escorting the trucks to their destination.

While they ate lunch, the ground crew refuelled the aircraft, checked that the cargo was securely lashed down and ensured that the plane was in good working order.

After two boring hours at the airport in the Siberian capital, the relief crew, who had been travelling with them, took over to fly the aircraft to its final destination, Magadan-Sokol International Airport, some fifty kilometres north of Magadan. This meant that, upon arrival, the goods would have to be unloaded from the plane, loaded back onto trucks and transported by road to the port city. After that, the shipment would be safely stored in a specially guarded hangar.

Oleg reflected that one of the advantages of this dismal wasteland at the end of the world was that the nearest town was more than two thousand three hundred kilometres away and could only be reached by a single carriageway that was highly unsuitable due to the state of the road... when there was a road, which was also not guaranteed.

While the cargo was being dropped off at the warehouses, they all went to the centre of Magadan to book a room at the Hotel Vm-Tsentral'naya. Oleg climbed into bed and fell asleep instantly. He was exhausted.

The next morning, he woke up full of energy. He had slept soundly and after a hearty breakfast he was ready to resume his journey.

He said goodbye to the men who had driven them there and went to retrieve the trucks that had been parked in the hangar.

Then he made his way with the line of trucks behind him to the port, where they were to load all the equipment into the bowels of the freighter. While the stevedores were doing their work, Oleg went to inspect his cabin. It was certainly nothing like the one on the yacht, but far superior to those of the rest of the crew, and probably on a par with the one the captain was using. He would have to live in that pit for the next eight days until they completed the almost eight thousand kilometres to their final destination of Hai Phong in Vietnam, so it was important. What's more, he had his own shower, unlike the sailors who had to share one amongst each other.

After a couple of hours of work the cargo was on board and well secured. Everything was ready for the long voyage. The first officer reported to the captain, who immediately called Oleg's cabin to inform him.

'Everything's ready, sir. We sail when you give the word.'

'Let's go, then, Captain!'

'First Officer, commence manoeuvres.'

And the ship with its deadly cargo undocked and set course for the port of Hai Phong in Vietnam. None of the crew knew the contents of those crates. The labels and the cargo manifest were totally false.

Oleg resolved to spend as much time as possible relaxing on his bunk. Outside, the wind, the cold and the rain did not tempt one to walk around the swaying, slippery deck. At the most, he could enjoy a hot cup of coffee in the restaurant lounge, provided he kept a firm grip on the mug to avoid it being knocked over by the tossing and turning of the ship.

As he tried to drink a nice cup of coffee, he watched the crew with a certain admiration and some pity. He couldn't understand how these people could endure such a quality of life, working in harsh conditions, for ridiculous wages and living in quarters that were moving in all directions all the time. They risked their lives on every voyage, exposed to the onslaught of the sea and tossed by each pounding wave. The cargo could break loose, destabilise the ship and sink it in a matter of seconds.

He watched the way they moved about. They had become so adapted to the unsteady, ever-changing environment that walking with their legs apart and making continuous compensatory movements to maintain their balance had become second nature, something they did unconsciously.

Oleg was not used to such rough seas as those of Okhotsk. He had spent years sailing serenely in the calm Mediterranean, which, from time to time, became choppy, but never as rough as this. A pleasure boat was one thing, but a large cargo ship was another. The first two days were not the best he had ever spent at sea. But between the Dramamine tablets and the alcohol, he managed to withstand the assault.

From time to time, he would go up to the bridge to chat with the captain and officers. They were used to the rough weather and would joke about his lack of sea legs. From the bridge the view was spectacular. Through the window Oleg could see the prow of the ship sinking to depths from which it seemed impossible to emerge, and when it did, half the ocean would break against the glass of the windows, after having scoured the deck and added another layer of ice to whatever was exposed to the elements.

Oleg asked where they were, more or less, and the first officer answered in latitude and longitude.

'What's that in layman's terms?'

'Ah! Sorry. About halfway.'

'That's great, thanks.'

At that moment, from the bowels of the ship, a tremendous, roar rose up to the bridge, as deafening alarms and sirens began to sound and all kinds of emergency warning lights started to flash. Despite the excitement and the noise, the crew remained calm as if they were listening to the news on the radio. No one uttered an exclamation, no one shouted, no one showed any sign of being overwhelmed by the circumstances. But everyone had their entire attention focused on what was happening.

'What's going on?' Oleg asked aghast.

'Apparently there's been an explosion in the cargo hold. We have a major leak,' replied the captain as he continued to issue orders to contain the leak and isolate the hold.

'An explosion?'

'It would seem so, sir. Excuse me, I have to give this my full attention.'

Two minutes later, the captain took the microphone and addressed the crew.

'Launch the lifeboats. Abandon ship. Repeat, abandon ship.'

33.   The sabotage

The explosions in the ship's cargo hold were only the beginning of the inferno that was unleashed in the deep recesses of the vessel.

The breach that opened up quickly began to flood the ship with a huge influx of icy water. The explosions caused the cargo straps to snap so that the load shifted, which in turn caused the ship to keel over with no chance of recovering its position. The fire then ignited the ammunition and gunpowder, like a mini war taking place inside the hold, with bullets of all calibres flying in all directions, and these explosions further aggravated the already desperate situation of the ship, filling the hull with holes through which, in turn, even more water entered. The hold became a veritable sieve.

The captain had just enough time to launch an SOS and order everyone to abandon ship in the lifeboats.

The saboteur who pressed the switch to detonate the bomb was on deck and was among the first to launch a boat and get inside.

The lifeboats were fully enclosed and could hold half a dozen people each. They survived the inclement weather in them until they were picked up by another boat in the area, that had heard the SOS.

Fortunately, there were no fatalities. There were only a few minor injuries, some of them from gunshot wounds, which was a surprise to the crew, but not to Oleg.

The ship, along with all its cargo, lay foundered beneath the frozen waters of the Sea of Okhotsk. Operation SAMARIO had failed.

34.   The mole exposed

The system of communication between Inspector Encinas and his secret informer had been very neat, but the time had come to go a step further and move beyond its limitations. He needed to establish direct, face-to-face communication. And he also needed to talk to Marina, the nightclub waitress. She had vanished without trace and he needed to talk to her, if it turned out that she was still in Spain. And this is what he told his informer. But when he got the answer, he went cold:

They are watching me all the time. We can't be seen together. Certainly not at the police station.

So, 'M' was Marina, the waitress? Had he been in contact with her all this time without knowing it? He didn't know why he had come up with the idea that the informer was a man and someone from within the police force. It would never have occurred to him that it could be a woman, let alone her. He now understood the difficulty of having a face-to-face meeting, and yet he needed to talk to her, but without using such inconvenient technology. That system of leaving messages in the draft folder was fine for illicit love affairs, but now something more professional was needed. That's when he decided it was time to move up a notch.

If you are the only one who has access to your personal computer, install this software. It's one hundred percent secure. We can chat without the risk of anyone knowing what we're talking about. I'll be waiting for you on the other side of the link.

Without a mobile phone properly configured for secure conversations, it was the best solution. Moreover, for Marina, working so closely with Oleg, to have two mobile phones would have immediately aroused suspicion and her life would have been worth nothing.

All that remained was for Marina to have sufficient competence to be able to install the software Encinas was proposing. It wasn't complicated, but some people were very inept. Something told him, however, that Marina wasn't one of them.

Fermín Encinas was connected to the app just as he had promised her. He waited for what seemed like an interminable period of time. He was gripped by anxiety and doubts: would she be able to install it without problems? would she have second thoughts, fearing the consequences? had she accidently deleted it? had she been discovered? would he finally discover that it had all been a delaying tactic and a hoax? Was she being monitored at that moment and could not express herself freely? Was she acting as a double agent? While Fermín was lost in all this agonizing, he noticed that something was changing on his computer screen. Marina was online. He celebrated with a sip of his favourite whisky that he had poured himself when he got home to help him unwind.

'I'm here, Inspector Encinas.'

'Hi, good to talk to you, thanks for all your help.'

After the initial greeting, Fermín had dozens of questions he wanted to ask Marina. He had to organize his thoughts so as not to overwhelm her.

'I'm going to pass on the information I've gathered up to this point. You can corroborate it later, OK?'

'OK.'

From that moment on, Marina's fingers flew over the keyboard providing a wealth of information and very useful details. Some of these details had been previously verified by the investigation, which provided irrefutable proof of their reliability.

Marina identified Oleg, her lover, as the one responsible for organising the whole operation, although the mastermind was Ivan Orlov, under the direct supervision of President Igor Ruskin.

This was something very big and far beyond the competence of a simple policeman, even if he was a CNI agent. There were implications for the state and too many important people involved up to their necks.

Marina provided dates on which Ivan, Oleg and Ruskin met at the huge mansion that Ruskin owned in La Zagaleta, a deluxe, exclusive residential development near the town of Benahavis, in Malaga.

Ruskin's house had a private heliport, so he was able to come to Spain and be transferred to his villa completely unobserved by members of the general public.

'But why all the rigmarole, the robbery, the murders of the guards, why are the top guys involved in something so messy?'

'The burglary operation was just a way to finance the manufacture of an arsenal.'

'And what's the arsenal for? Don't they have enough weapons already?'

'The operation is divided into several phases. The first, the burglary. The second, the sale of the artwork. The third, the manufacture of the weapons. The fourth, the transportation of the weapons.'

'Where are the weapons going? To start a new war?'

'The weapons are going to Vietnam.'

'Vietnam?!!! What for? It's a friendly country.'

'The ultimate aim of this whole operation, designed by the Russian FSB, is to take over a mine containing a very rare mineral which is extremely valuable due to its unique properties.'

'And the mine is in Vietnam?'

'Yes. In fact it has the second largest reserves of this mineral in the world.'

'And what mineral is it? What's in it?'

'It's SAMARIUM.'

'That means nothing to me. It's the first time I've heard of it.'

'Samarium is in the Lanthanide series of metallic chemical elements and is present in samarskite, but also in cerite, ortite, ytterbite, gadolinite, bastnasite, monazite and many other minerals besides. The last two are currently its main sources. It's separated from them by solvent extraction using ionic liquid, and, more recently, by electrochemical deposition. The largest reserves are found in China, Vietnam, Brazil, Russia, South Africa, India, Australia and the USA, with China being the world's largest producer.'

My God, she's one hell of a cocktail waitress! thought Fermín, who was astounded by Marina's mastery of the subject.

'OK, you've impressed me, but what's it used for?'

'Samarium is among other things an additive in the control rods of nuclear reactors (the isotope Sm-149 is a good neutron absorber). Given its importance and the reserves in other countries, it follows that Russia can't afford to be at the mercy of the vagaries of politics or the market for rare materials.'

'But there's one thing I don't understand. Vietnam is a friendly country - why the weapons?'

'The objective is to defend by all possible means the extraction of the ore from the mine, which is located in Vietnamese territory, but only a short distance from the border with China, in a very mountainous area. In theory, it's always possible that China might want more than it already has, and Vietnamese politicians and military personnel are not exactly renowned for their loyalty and honesty. So, the operation was aimed at ensuring the supply of this material was one hundred per cent secure.'

'OK, I see. Do you know why the guards were killed in Marbella? Did something go wrong?'

'Oleg had bribed the shift leader and the guards, but they got greedy and Oleg gave the order to eliminate them.'

'And now comes the million-dollar question: who did it?'

'The mole. That giant mole in your garden.'

'Do you know his name?'

For a few interminable seconds the cursor on the screen blinked, waiting for Marina to provide the name. And when she decided to write it down, Fermín's world came crashing down on him.

'Jesús Frutos.'

Fermín sat with his mouth open and the glass of whisky in his hand, reading over and over again the name Marina had written. He couldn't swallow another sip of his whisky and put the glass back on the table.

'It can't be. It must be a frame-up or something. Sometimes I've begun to suspect a little incompetence, but this is way too much.'

'No. The superintendent has for some time now been collaborating with Ivan Orlov, directly.'

'Why?'

'Why d'you think? For money. Frutos is close to retirement and had some financial problems. He had maintenance to pay to his ex-wives and in addition, he had some gambling problems. He started to get into debt. They met each other at an event organised by a company dedicated to bringing the Russian community and the

Spanish community together. And then Ivan realised that he had a gold mine. He solved Frutos' money problems in a discreet way, making luck "smile" on him in the poker games that were organised at the casino and Frutos secured himself a decent retirement. Or so he thought.'

'And it was he who eliminated the guards? I can't believe it.'

'Ivan had him by the balls. He couldn't say no. He had to do it or the next one to disappear would be him.'

'But the gun is known to have been part of a previous crime, also in Marbella, involving a member of a criminal gang. Was that him too?'

'Ivan has controlled him for a long time and was at loggerheads with the gang.'

Fermín was devastated. It was true that the CNI had placed him in that position to check what was going on. Apparently, there were certain doubts about the superintendent's attitude, but he never imagined it would come to this.

'I presume there's proof of what you're saying, is there?'

'Search his house and you'll find the Makarov you're looking for.'

'Do you know who ordered the copy of the key to Bukowski's villa?'

'The housekeeper, Guadalupe. She sleeps with Frutos from time to time.'

He was devastated yet at the same time satisfied. He had the explanation to all the mysteries that had been baffling him, but he never thought he would have to blow the whistle on someone as high up as the chief superintendent.

'Oleg told you everything?'

'There's nothing like having sex with someone to loosen their tongue.'

'I'll bear that in mind. Thanks very much, Marina. Now I'd better report all this to my superiors.'

35.   The demise of the mole

At four o'clock in the morning on a cold day in early December, a large police deployment, under the command of the Chief of Police of Andalusia, appeared with the necessary search warrant at the home of Superintendent Jesús Frutos.

The police stormed into his house en masse, breaking the lock with a hefty battering ram, accompanied by shouts of *Freeze, police*!

They went straight to the bedroom where they expected, given the time of day, he would be sleeping. And it was then that they found the superintendent's dead body.

He was sitting with his back against the headboard of the bed. The wall behind him was splattered with blood and there was a bullet hole in his right temple. Next to him on the bed, a Makarov pistol fitted with a silencer completed the tragic scene.

> 'Place that gun in a bag and cover him up,' ordered the Chief of Police and one of the police officers hastened to use the sheets and the duvet to carry out the order.
>
> 'Sir! Come and take a look at this,' shouted another from the living room.

On top of the hall table was an unsealed envelope addressed 'To the Coroner'. Inside were some typed sheets of paper, and on the last one, the signature of the deceased.

My name is Jesús Frutos Labandeira.

I have decided to put an end to my life, tired of having to look at myself in the mirror every morning and of not being able to bear what I see.

I ask forgiveness from all those I have harmed and those who have felt betrayed by me.

The letter then went on to confess to a whole series of crimes and misdemeanours he had committed over the years. He also indicated that it had been Ivan Orlov who had ensnared him and forced him to do terrible things in exchange for sparing his life, but that he had reached a point where he no longer wanted to live like that.

They also found a safe hidden behind the bookcase. It was open. Inside were a multitude of folders with documentation taken from the police station referring to various cases that had remained unsolved, mostly related to Ivan and the Russians.

I was the one who drew the plan of the house so that they could find the picture. Its owner, Bukowski, had invited me to one of his dinners and because of my knowledge of art I came up with the idea of taking it. I promised Guadalupe that we would enjoy the spoils in the Caribbean. Then Ivan found out and changed the plan completely.

I duped Guadeloupe. I made her believe I was in love with her. That way it was easier to convince her to make a copy of the key to the front door.

I have been regularly informing Ivan Orlov of the progress of the investigations into this case, which made it possible for Oleg to get away.

'I never imagined that a police officer could sink so low,' said the chief with a disgusted look on his face. It's one thing to fence dope or tobacco but it's another to become a thug, while still wearing the uniform. A murderous thug, and for a foreigner on top of that.'

He took a deep breath, before continuing.

'The official report will say that Superintendent Frutos suffered a tragic accident while cleaning his service weapon and died when he shot himself by mistake.

Nothing should be leaked to the press about the existence of this letter. The same goes for these folders.

If the superintendent's morals left a lot to be desired, making them public would be detrimental to all of us, regardless of whether we are saints or not. That's the pitfall of wearing this uniform: that the sins of one man can taint the entire force.'

36.   The evidence against "the mole"

Fermín Encinas was really upset when he found out that the infamous mole within the police, who was collaborating with Ivan Orlov and Oleg Sokolov, was Chief Superintendent Jesús Frutos himself. And there was worse to come.

The day after his confidential conversation with Marina - now he knew it had been her all along - he received a call from his colleagues in charge of monitoring the CNI. Since they had installed microphones and hidden cameras and hacked into the mobile phones, 99% of the information was not relevant to the investigation. But there was one exception and it was time to share that intel with him.

Encinas already knew who the mole was, but he only had the testimony of a person who had never spoken directly to Frutos. It was a statement based on information from a third person, information she had obtained by sharing a bed with a foreign spy.

In a trial, they would be on very thin ice and with an astute lawyer the case could easily fall apart. In addition, the letter found in Frutos' home could be a false trail left by the actual murderers to convince the police that it was suicide. This would complicate the investigation since they would have to establish whether it was a murder disguised as a suicide or a real one.

When they called him from the CNI office in Marbella, he was still hoping to resolve these questions. Because he still had some loose ends and some doubts that the letter and Marina's inside information had not entirely cleared up.

One of these was the question of who the woman was who had ordered the key that allowed them entry into the house. It had to be one of the household staff. He had to prove that, as Marina had said, it was Guadalupe, the housekeeper. He needed proof that Frutos and Guadalupe were in a relationship.

And the other important aspect was to identify the real killers - or killer, according to his secret informant - of the security guards. That was yet another piece of information Marina had given him that needed to be confirmed. The police knew that the bullets had come from a Russian-made gun, a Makarov, which had already been used in other crimes, but not who had been in possession of it.

When he reached the undercover office, a location hidden behind the name of a company purporting to be hiring out private jets, he greeted his colleagues and his boss.

'Hi, Encinas. How's it going? Follow me, please.'

The officer in charge took him to a blacked out room where they had already set up a projection screen and a whole array of audiovisual equipment, including a projector. Controlling all of this was a young police officer in civilian clothes.

'Put on your headphones and pay attention to what you are about to hear and see. This is the result of your brilliant plan to keep everyone involved under surveillance.'

Next, video footage was projected onto the wall. Encinas recognised Frutos' vehicle and his house. The superintendent was driving his car and was accompanied by a woman. The car was entering the garage of Frutos' house.

'Fast-forward.' the officer in charge ordered the operator.

Immediately, at the bottom of the screen, the clock advanced by eight hours and the date moved forward. It was the morning of the next day.

In the video an Uber taxi pulled up at the front door of the house and stopped to wait.

'Watch carefully, Encinas, do you recognise that woman?'

From inside the house, a woman could be seen coming out of the front door, walking towards the taxi and getting into it. Encinas now had confirmation of the information that Marina had given him.

'Yes, her name is Guadalupe and she is the housekeeper of the robbery victim.'

'She spent the night with Superintendent Frutos, the head of the investigation,' he said aloud so that it would be reflected in the audio that was being recorded and would form part of the formal criminal charge.

Encinas, while relieved that the matter was being resolved, was also devastated. It was one thing to think that the superintendent had too many failings and deserved to be retired for incompetence, and another to have irrefutable proof that he was a traitor and a murderer.

'We can deduce,' the CNI chief continued, 'that it was she who, on Frutos' instructions, made a copy of the key so that the robbery could be carried out. It is less important who physically handed over the key. She needs to be arrested and interrogated.'

'I'll take care of it,' said Encinas. 'Can I use this footage?'

'Not at the moment, no. I'm sorry, but you may say that we have it.'

'Understood. Anything else?'

'Yes, there is.'

The chief signalled to the operator. He manipulated the controls of the equipment and a conversation could be heard through the headphones. One of the voices was that of Frutos. The other had a strong eastern accent. They were talking on the phone from the superintendent's house.

'Things are getting very complicated, Ivan. This is not what we agreed.'

'Haven't you received your money in Switzerland?'

'Yes, but that was for the robbery. Not for taking care of those two poor bastards.'

'Those poor bastards, as you call them, wanted to blackmail me! Me! Ivan Orlov! I couldn't allow it.'

'Yes, but that was a matter for you, for your pride and your ego. There was no need for you to involve me.'

The chief gestured again and the audio stopped.

'There's more, but I think that's enough.'

Encinas, with his head down, feeling awkward and uncomfortable that he had uncovered and confirmed who the mole was, did not feel the satisfaction of having fulfilled his mission. He felt a sense of defeat at the realisation of how weak human beings can be, even to the point of turning into real vermin. And he prayed that he would never sink so low.

'What now?'

'We have already issued a special arrest warrant. In the next few hours there will be a major police operation aimed at arresting the superintendent, searching his home, the housekeeper's house, his office and everything he has had access to. Congratulations on your splendid work!' he said as he reached out to shake hands with him.

'Thank you, sir,' Encinas reciprocated the gesture.

'You don't look pleased, Encinas.'

'Would you be, sir?'

'The bad guys are always bad regardless of whether or not they wear a uniform and despite what uniform they wear. There always have been and there always will be bad apples. The important thing is to find them. It's a shame we couldn't save the lives of those two unfortunate security guards.'

'Yes, that's another way of looking at it. At least now, we can call off the surveillance.'

'Including that of your friend Eduardo Navarro.'

'Yeah. I'm none too proud of that, I must say.'

'It was the right thing to do, Encinas. And you did it. That's what this job is all about. Doing the right thing even if nobody sees us.'

Encinas stood up. He didn't know where to go. He didn't feel like going back to the police station. He didn't want to run into Frutos, knowing that in a few hours he would be arrested. He didn't want to see Eduardo since although his colleague was unaware of it, he felt he had betrayed their friendship.

'Thank you for everything, sir. Thank you for your support and your help.'

'Thank you, Encinas. You are a good officer, a good policeman and most importantly, a good person. Don't let the environment change you so much that you don't recognise yourself.'

'I'll try.'

'What are you going to do now? Where are you going?'

'To arrest Guadalupe and interrogate her.'

'Do that. If you need to get drunk later, call me. Somebody's got to drive.'

'I'll bear that in mind, sir.'

'Take care of yourself.'

'Thank you, sir. You too.'

37. Daniel Olavarría: Mission accomplished

After Interpol arrested Mahfuz Amirmoez on official charges of art trafficking, Commander Carmen Riviera de las Torras y Grande Benjumea remained with her colleagues to finish the operation. She had an ace up her sleeve. She would threaten the trafficker with charges of complicity in the murder of two people in an attempt to get him to cooperate with Interpol and not only confess to all the works of questionable provenance he had, but also to give them the names of his main suppliers or sellers. She was sure that more than one well-known name with a good public image in the art world would be dragged through the mud, among them, the Belgian.

Daniel, for his part, once he had the work of art in his possession, thanked her for her help and headed for the airport, where the crew of the jet was waiting for him, as had been arranged on his departure from the hotel.

After six long hours of flying, they landed back home in Malaga. Daniel said a warm farewell to the crew and they agreed to organise a dinner in a restaurant together. They even set a date, time and place. When he got off the plane, naturally, Bukowski had put his chauffeur and his car at his service. Daniel had the impression that when he had to drive his own car again, he wouldn't be satisfied until he had bought himself something classier.

'Sir, have you heard the news?'

'I haven't seen the papers yet. What's happened?'

'Chief Superintendent Frutos, from the Marbella police, has been found dead at his home. Apparently, he had an accident while cleaning his gun.'

'I mention it because Mr Bukowski thought you might be interested. He said you were friends.'

Daniel was aghast. He couldn't imagine that his friend Frutos had been careless with his gun. Dead! He couldn't believe it. And yet he was.

'Yes, we were friends,' was his taciturn response to the chauffer.

Suddenly he realised that he was struggling with conflicting emotions. He was pleased with his tour of Europe and the Middle East, which had enabled him to recover the stolen drawing in record time. And just when he was ready to celebrate with champagne, he had unexpectedly learned of the death of his friend the superintendent. The news had soured his initial enthusiasm.

He had managed to recover the picture through a combination of circumstances and good luck. Playing on people's greed, inciting and provoking traffickers and unscrupulous people. In this way he had succeeded in getting the Belgian to take the bait and in the process had also got the scumbag Mahfuz Amirmoez on the hook. Only a fool like him would dream of having on display all the pieces of art he had bought without having taken the precaution of checking their authenticity.

And yet now, instead of feeling satisfied and happy for having fulfilled his promise, he had to hear this tragic news.

The Lord giveth and the Lord taketh away, he thought.

But life goes on. So, there he was, in Bukowski's car, on his way to his villa to give him back what had always been his. And at no extra cost, except for the hotel bills, the plane, the helicopters, the chauffeurs and the limousines. Dinners and drinks he had paid for out of his own pocket. He felt indebted to Bukowski.

It is true that, throughout his career as a private detective, he had always been driven by a desire to safeguard objects of art, but he could not ignore the fact that money had always been a great incentive. It had allowed him to enjoy a life full of pleasures and luxuries within the reach of very few. But that had been until that moment.

For some reason that he had not yet been able to explain to himself, on this occasion he had not really been motivated by money, even if that was what had prompted him to accept the assignment. He had felt something deep inside and had done it for other reasons. Perhaps it was to compensate for the terrible experiences his client - a respected, polite, kind and generous old man - had been subjected to. If he retrieved the sketch, he might perhaps give him one last bit of joy in his life. For all his immense wealth, he was without doubt a lonely man, clearly with very influential acquaintances and contacts, but perhaps without any true friends. And certainly no family, who had been wiped out by the Nazis. All this, together with his poor health, had created an image of vulnerability in Daniel's mind that he was unable to blot out.

As he arrived at the main entrance to the villa, he had the impression that several years had passed since the last time he was there. Everything had unfolded so rapidly that it was difficult to process so many events in such a short period of time.

Tomas, the butler, greeted him with a broad smile and led him into the office where Aaron Bukowski was waiting for him. Rising from his chair, he went to shake Daniel's hand and looking him straight in the eye he uttered a brief but succinct:

'Thank you.'

Daniel thought he could see a twinkle in the man's eyes. And when he took the Dürer self-portrait out of his briefcase and handed it to him, he realised that the twinkle was in fact the old man's tears.

He took the masterpiece in his hands as if it might break. He held it close to his chest and it became clear that he was the one who was breaking, standing in the middle of his office, unable to utter a word or move.

Daniel, too, was overcome with emotion and a lump rose up in his throat. It was never a pleasant sight to see a person cry, but the tears of an old man were especially distressing.

After a few moments of silence, which seemed an eternity, Bukowski seemed to regain his composure. He calmed down, placed the work of art inside its original frame and hung it back in its place, as if nothing had happened. Once it was back on the wall, he stood quietly contemplating the drawing, no doubt remembering the thousands of images it evoked from his childhood.

Once he had recovered his breath and his peace of mind, he suddenly turned back to Daniel, as if he had forgotten he was there.

'Oh, Daniel my friend, I beg your pardon. I was overcome by the emotion of the moment and my reaction to it. Forgive this poor sentimental old man.'

'You have nothing to apologise for, believe me. I'm glad I was able to carry out the assignment successfully. The truth is that it looked pretty bleak at first, but I had a bit of luck.'

'Would you like something to drink?'

'A coffee?'

'Haha, I was thinking of something stronger,' he said with a mischievous smile, as he pulled a bottle of Macallan whisky and two glasses out of his desk drawer. 'Let's raise a glass, Daniel my friend, to decent people and to friends.'

'To decent people and to friends.'

And they both knocked back the restorative dram of whisky that he had poured out.

'What are your plans now, Daniel?'

'To take a break, which I had already planned to do before you convinced me to get involved in this affair.'

'Do you have family?'

'No. I haven't led a very conventional life, always travelling about and just living for the moment. Nor have I ever met the woman who might make me reconsider my situation. I have met many, most of them superfluous, manipulative, scheming, egotistical, self-serving and even murderous. Perhaps it has been this image that has marked me when it comes to committing myself.'

'You must have met some that were worth knowing, surely?'

For a few seconds he seemed to be reflecting and reaching far back into the past. Or perhaps he wanted to hide the effect that some of these women had had on his life.

'Yes, but either she was already happily married, or she was simply married even if she wasn't happy, or she was a lesbian.'

'Haha. It sounds like you've had no luck on that front, my friend Daniel.'

'Maybe I'm just too demanding.'

'The time has come to reward your hard work as it merits, Daniel.'

'Look, Mr Bukowski, I've been thinking about it and I have to say that after all your kindness and generosity, I wouldn't feel comfortable accepting payment now.'

'Why not? It's only right.'

'Mr Bukowski, I have flown halfway round the world in your plane, stayed in your hotels, used your cars and your chauffeurs, and you even provided helicopters to fly me between Nice and Monte Carlo. What kind of person would now have the audacity to present you with a bill? I can't do that, sir. I'm sorry, I don't mean to insult you, please don't take it badly. It's just that my conscience won't allow it.'

'I wouldn't like to trouble your conscience, my friend Daniel, but if that's the way it is, would you allow me to invite you to a dinner I am organising here at home with some friends. Do please come.'

'Of course. It would be my pleasure. Thank you very much.'

'By the way: don't even think of bringing wine or champagne. I have a well-stocked cellar.'

'I'm sure you have, sir. I can believe it.'

'Very well, then. I'll call you when I've got it organised.'

'Perfect. What will the dress code be?'

'Wear whatever you want, jeans if you like. I just need you to come.'

'I will.'

38.   Operation *Babel*

As soon as the CNI found out through its agent Marina what Oleg and his men were planning to do, things started to move unusually quickly at the international level.

It was an operation fraught with difficulties, particularly given the diplomatic status enjoyed by Ivan Orlov. So, an operation was designed to obstruct him, but indirectly.

To attack "the Russian" directly would be borderline suicidal. However, the same ends could be achieved by sabotaging the delivery of arms to Vietnam. But it had to be done before they reached Vietnam, because of the same political implications. Therefore, the attack would have to be made on the high seas, against the ship transporting them.

Several countries had a vested interest in Russia not having more control over such a sensitive, rare and scarce mineral. Not least, Vietnam itself, which owned the mine and had huge reserves.

The Vietnamese security forces were shocked to learn of the intentions of their Russian friends and how they had managed to corrupt the entire military leadership, together with all the customs and trade officials. Furthermore, the Chinese were not pleased to learn that they intended to grab the ore from a mine in Vietnamese territory which was situated only a short distance from the Chinese border. Indeed, the Chinese attitude was that the material belonged more to them than to the Russians anyway.

Needless to say, the USA were totally against the idea, although the difference, in their case, was that the Americans advocated that none of those named so far should have any of the mineral.

Consequently, by combining the interests of several countries, it was not difficult to sabotage the Samarium operation which the Russians were carrying out. This led to the intervention being given the name Operation *Babel*.

Initially, various alternatives were considered. Some believed that the stopover in Novosibirsk was the ideal time to place an explosive in the cargo, but blowing it up on Russian territory was politically very risky. If this was to be avoided, it would have to be detonated by means of a delay mechanism, which complicated matters considerably, but was not impossible.

Other theories suggested that the best place to introduce a bomb was at the port of Magadan. In which case, the problem was that if the device was discovered, or failed, there was no room for manoeuvre to rectify the situation. Some suggested torpedoing the ship with a submarine, or with a missile, but after assessing the diplomatic risks, this proposal was discarded.

There were two aspects that were fundamental to the sabotage operation. One was the detonation mechanism of the bomb, and the other was that all the equipment had to be rendered useless. Exploding a bomb in Novosibirsk was not a 100% guarantee that all the equipment would be destroyed. And that was crucial. So, in the end, it was decided that the bomb should be exploded in the open sea and the weapons should be sent to the bottom of the ocean.

If they opted for a timing device, the ship might not be in deep enough water and then, even if the bomb exploded, the wreckage might not sink to a sufficient depth, favouring a subsequent salvage operation. In such a scenario, all they would achieve would be to delay delivery of the weapons. There would certainly be damage, but the aim was for both the ship and the weapons to end up on the seabed.

The other possibility was by remote control. With greater control over the timing, but much more dangerous for the lunatic who triggered it, because it meant that the operative would have to be inside the ship with the consequent risk to his own life.

In the end, a Solomonic decision was taken: in both Novosibirsk and Magadan, two devices would be introduced, each with a different initiation system. One with a timing device and the other with a remote control. Thus, it was expected that setting off the remote control with its corresponding explosion would provoke the destruction of the other device and vice versa. The ammunition and gunpowder would do the rest.

But who would be suicidal enough to risk his life to sink the ship he himself was travelling on? As it was a joint operation of several secret services, a sailor of Russian nationality, whose parents had been sent to forced labour camps, was eventually found. He was a secret sleeper agent who had remained inactive for years, waiting patiently to exact his revenge.

During the stopover that the Antonov An-225 made in the Siberian capital, a maintenance crew member was able to insert an explosive device with a timer. It was not overly powerful, but given the environment in which it would detonate, the cargo itself would do the rest.

The plan was that the operation would be a complete failure. In this way, Moscow would have to summon the much-loved Ivan for an explanation, since he was the one who had first refused to take responsibility for leading the operation and then suggested the name of Oleg, who, if all went according to plan, would also come out very badly because of his incompetence and negligence. In other words, they would kill several birds with one sinking. At the same time, they would also destroy the top tier of the organisation and the network of contacts they had set up on the Costa del Sol and would doubtless cause panic amongst those who had stayed behind. And lastly but no less important, it would prevent Russia from creating another quasi military skirmish, this time in Vietnam, to take control of a rare and very valuable mineral.

39.   The celebration

After the success of operation *Babel*, a private celebration was organised in the secret headquarters of the Spanish espionage services, attended by the heads of each sector.

The party was held in a spacious room, four levels below ground, where there was no possibility of external electronic surveillance.

Encinas knew some of his fellow officers as he had worked with them on other missions and was glad to see them and catch up with them. Then he went to say hello to the chief. As he was talking to him, he suddenly saw the most beautiful woman he had ever seen enter the room: Marina, the waitress at the club.

Seeing her there now, he realised that she too was a member of the CNI, although she had never mentioned anything about it to him. Suddenly, he felt like a fool and realised he had been manipulated by his boss and by her.

The chief turned his head to see what had caught Encinas' attention. Seeing her arrive, he beckoned her to come over. As she crossed the room and waved to one of her colleagues, there was a sudden hush, and all eyes were focused on her. Encinas couldn't stop staring at her, and she resolutely returned his gaze.

'Thank you very much for coming, Marina. I know you're not very fond of this sort of thing,' the chief greeted her. And then, looking at Encinas, he introduced them:

'Encinas, your partner Marina. Although I think you've already met, haven't you?'

'Yes, but then I didn't know we were working for the same side,' he said as he shook her hand. 'Besides,' he added 'she looked different.'

'Different?' she asked, a little surprised.

'Yes. That day you were in your waitress uniform and today you are looking magnificent. May I say, your perfume is exquisite.'

'Thank you, partner. And you don't need to be so formal, for goodness' sake. I know I'm very imposing in heels, but we can still be friends,' she said as she winked at him playfully.

And looking at their boss:

'Chief, we should have these parties more often. I love compliments,' she said with a huge smile on her face.

Fermín was sure he looked ridiculous and had the impression that he was drooling saliva out of his gaping mouth.

The chief handed each of them a glass of champagne and left them to it, walking over to a rostrum with a solitary microphone poised on its stand. The head of the Task Force was about to formally open the proceedings. He raised his glass of champagne and thanked his staff for their work. He also wanted to share the congratulations they had received from other secret services for the work they had done.

Encinas could not take his eyes off Marina. He was mesmerised by her exotic and spectacular beauty.

She, who had noticed his reaction, turned her face for a moment towards Encinas. She looked him in the eye and gave him a smile that would have melted the two poles of the Earth.

'If later the chief asks you what he said and you don't know, he'll send you to Siberia,' joked Marina.

'Would you like to live in Siberia?'

'Why do you think I live in Marbella, out of masochism?' she said as she widened her smile and showed her dazzling white teeth.

The operational chief spoke briefly. It was just an excuse to get the party started over cocktails, soft drinks and canapés. The perfect excuse for Encinas to chat with Marina. The first question was textbook.

'Marina.'

'Yes, Fermín.'

It was the first time he had heard her name on his lips and his heart skipped a beat and began to race at a hundred and thirty.

'How does a girl like you end up in a place like this.'

'It's rather a long story.'

'I have time and, above all, I'd really like to get to know more about you.'

'To begin with, I am not Russian. I'm Ukrainian. I was born in Kiev. I'm from a poor family. When I was young, I worked as a model. They were sporadic, casual jobs, nothing of great consequence, but they enabled me to help out my parents and pay for my studies at university.'

Fermín was totally enchanted by her slight accent, which made her even more charming, and by her delicate voice.

'After university....'

'What did you study?'

'Geology.'

'Hence the dissertation on Samarium that you gave me?'

'Yes. Haha.'

'Please, go on.'

'Well, after university, the truth is that I didn't have many employment opportunities. Time went by and I couldn't find any work in my area of expertise. I tried a number of companies connected to the oil industry, but with no luck. That's when I started to think about using modelling as my main source of income.'

'I don't understand why you didn't pursue that, Marina. I've never seen a more beautiful woman in my life.'

As he said it, he allowed his gaze to lose itself in her huge emerald-green eyes. She'd heard many honeyed words given as compliments, but this one sounded sincere. It wasn't the typical flattery whose only purpose was to get her into bed. It had come from Inspector Encinas' soul.

'Well, believe it or not, the modelling world isn't all it's cracked up to be. And besides, there are girls much prettier than me. Trust me, I've seen them. In the end I was either too tall, too fat, had bandy legs or whatever. Besides, you wouldn't believe the things I've seen in the dressing rooms. The girls would often faint or have blackouts, usually due to low blood pressure or addiction to drugs and so on. Some girls, in order to maintain their skinny sizes, committed real barbarities and some even succumbed to bulimia. Not forgetting, of course, the invitations to become a luxury "escort" that were the order of the day. It was then that I decided to leave all that in Ukraine and come to Spain, to the Costa del Sol. I tried, of course, to make it here as a model. I thought my looks were different from what was common here.'

'I can vouch for that,' Fermín commented.

And she continued.

'I knew that it was always difficult to get started and I spent day after day walking around agencies with my portfolio book under my arm. But I had to earn a crust and so I contacted a company in Marbella that organises events to put Russian companies in contact with Spaniards.

'I know the company,' said Fermín. '*Destellos Marbella*, right?'

'Yes, that's the one.'

'Well, like most girls, I became a waitress. I quickly learned Spanish. At least I had a job. The rest came later.'

'And it was at one of those events that you met Oleg?'

'Yes. He noticed me, flirted with me, and helped me financially. I'm not an idiot and I knew what he wanted, but I needed money. And he had a lot of it. It was a commercial transaction. Besides, this way I could still help my parents, who were having a hard time in Kiev.'

'I totally get that. Go on.'

'That was the situation, but I had no idea who Oleg was. How he made his money.

One day I was having a coffee on the terrace, enjoying the weather and minding my own business and a couple approached me. Very naturally and politely they asked permission to sit at the table and chat with me. They started talking about modelling and so on, but soon the conversation drifted on to other things. Suddenly, they surprised me. They knew everything about me. Where I was born, about my parents, about Oleg... In the end, they were the ones who told me who the real Oleg was and what he did for a living. And they asked me if I was intending to continue the relationship.

At first, I was scared, but they quickly reassured me. They told me that they were "the good guys" and that they were very interested in me working with them, but incognito. That I didn't need to change anything, that I should continue with Oleg. In return, I should keep them up to date with everything I knew, everything Oleg shared with me and what I could find out. They, in exchange, would send money every month directly to my parents in Kiev, and they would also deposit the same amount in a joint account to which I had access, here in Spain. In this way my name would be shielded.'

'And that's my story, Inspector Encinas,' the last part of the sentence she said with a wry smile.

'Would you like another drink?'

'Yes. And something to eat. I'm hungry.'

Fermín approached the bar and ordered a couple of glasses of champagne. He gave one to Marina and a waiter passed by with a tray of freshly made croquettes.

'Scrummy, I love these!' she said, eating one in a single mouthful.

'Wow, you really are hungry.'

'Now it's your turn. What's your story?'

'My story is not as colourful as yours. I studied law and I set my heart on a master's degree in criminology. When I finished, I joined the police and almost immediately I was contacted by the CNI. Then one day I was sent to Marbella. They suspected something, but they didn't tell me what it was, and I don't suppose they expected it to be something quite so disgraceful.'

After taking a sip, Fermín asked her:

'When we were at the club *Irina*, did you already know who I was?'

'Haha. Yes.'

'So that means that *you* were given the correct information!'

'Yes, I was. That's the advantage of being a girl, hahaha.'

'So, what now? What about Oleg?'

'Oleg is history. He's lucky to have survived the shipwreck. He'll spend the rest of his life in a shitty basement office, in a room with no windows. And he can thank his lucky stars to be there and not in a worse place.'

'What about you? Aren't you afraid they'll look for you now that you have no one to protect you?'

'No. Nobody knows who I am. I was just Oleg's lover, the boss's mistress. That's the advantage of working surrounded by a bunch of male chauvinist pigs.'

40.   EPILOGUE

Ivan Orlov was enjoying his new-found retirement in his luxurious Marbella villa. As he lounged by the pool, soaking up the sun, one of the servants approached him with a tray.

'Sir, I have an urgent telegram.'
"The Russian" jolted himself out of his reverie. Between the sun and the alcohol he was drinking, he had been half asleep. He took the telegram, assuming it was confirmation that the Samarium operation had achieved its objectives.

Transport ship, sunk. Stop.
Sabotage. Stop.
Operation Samarium aborted. Stop.
Return immediately to Moscow to explain.

***

Oleg and the rest of the crew were rescued a few hours later by a fishing vessel that was in the area and heard the captain's SOS.

The rescue boat provided them with dry clothes and a place to sleep. They were cramped together due to the limited space, but at least they were still alive and they were dry.

Given the situation in which they were picked up, the captain decided to interrupt his fishing operations and take the survivors to a safe harbour and then continue with his more profitable haul.

The owner of the fishing vessel radioed this to the maritime authorities as soon as he confirmed that those rescued were well, except for some gunshot wounds, something that the captain of the cargo ship would later have to explain when he presented himself to the authorities.

The nearest port was Korsakov on Sakhalin Island. The captain of the rescue ship took advantage of the trip and, in addition to unloading the passengers, also unloaded the bumper catch he had landed, which almost filled the ship's holds with salmon, herring, haddock and cod.

Once they arrived safely in port, they had to present themselves at the marine command to report the incident and explain, among other things, what had happened and why there were crew members with gunshot wounds.

After giving their statements, the authorities handed Oleg a telegram addressed to him:

Return immediately to Moscow.
Full report of events required.

***

Vasili and Grigori, as had been agreed with superintendent Frutos, were still being held in Alhaurín prison in an isolation unit to protect them from the wrath of Ivan Orlov, Oleg and their henchmen.

Their life was rather monotonous, but they lived very well. They had never lived so comfortably in their lives, let alone in a prison. If only they had known, they would have done something to get inside a lot sooner.

They had been provided with a TV for their cell, had access to the prison swimming pool, were kept separate from the other inmates and generally felt like they were on holiday.

'You know what's starting to worry me, Vasili?'

'I have no idea. Surprise me.'

'That we're going to get used to living like this and we won't want to leave. This is like an all-expenses paid holiday.'

'For the time being, Grigori, we're safe here. You don't know what's waiting for you out there.'

'My girl is waiting for me. And yours is waiting for you too.'

Vasili suddenly felt a deep sense of longing. It was true that he missed his girlfriend, although he was trying hard not to torment himself with thoughts of her. He was trying to convince himself that, when he got out, she would no longer be there. Or if she was, she wouldn't want to be with a jobless no-hoper. He would have to look for work again. His friend's comments were certainly very ill-timed.

Suddenly, a prison officer with whom they had started to build a rapport, approached them.

'Basilio, Gregorio,' the guard had Hispanicized their names from the first day and they readily accepted it. 'You have a visitor.'

They were both very surprised and began to suspect that it might be a trick of Oleg's boys to get at them. They had no choice but to find out.

The officer escorted them into the visitor's room, guarded by two others, where Encinas was sitting at a table waiting for them. They remembered him from when they had come out of hiding and he had interrogated them.

'Good morning,' Encinas said.

'Good morning, Inspector,' they both replied as they sat down across from him.

'I have good news.'

Vasili and Grigori looked at each other in astonishment.

'Now, where shall I start? Oleg Sokolov has survived a shipwreck in the Sea of Okhotsk. He's reportedly being recalled to Moscow.

I suspect he will never return to Spain.'

They both smiled broadly. Their lives no longer seemed to be in so much danger.

'There's more. Superintendent Frutos...Superintendent Frutos has died. A fatal accident while handling his service weapon.'

At this news their expressions changed and they both looked distinctly upset and worried. The person with whom they had negotiated their surrender and their special status in prison was no longer there.

'On a separate matter, the stolen picture has been recovered and the buyer has been arrested. Given all these circumstances, I asked the judge handling your case to take into consideration your contrition, your spontaneous collaboration and your situation of vulnerability in the face of threats from assassins.'

Vasili and Grigori could not believe what they were hearing. A policeman speaking on their behalf to a judge - unbelievable! But they didn't want to interrupt him, lest they break the spell.

'I have therefore formally requested your conditional release pending trial. It's possible that it will take some time for a date to be set, given the delays in the justice system. During this time, you will have to report to the duty court every fortnight, you will not be allowed to leave the country, and if you wish to change your place of residence, you will have to give prior written notice. If you agree, please sign here.'

'What do we do to tell them that we are going to live in Rota?' Grigori asked immediately.

'I have another question, inspector,' Vasili interjected, 'How are we going to find work now that we have a record?'

'We've thought of that too. Taking into account the favourable reports from the prison authorities about your behaviour, we will provide you with a certificate that will prevent that from being an obstacle in your search for a job. Use it only if necessary. Ordinarily, nobody will ask you what you have been doing these past few months. In any case, you can say that you have been collaborating with the security forces, in something secret.'

'Why are you doing this, Inspector?' Vasili asked.

Fermín Encinas remained quiet for a few moments, looking at each of them, while he tried to figure out the answer.

'The judge asked me the same question. And I gave him the same answer I will give you: If you're not given a second chance, it's very likely that in the end you'll end up on a path that can only lead to misery. Believe me, I have personal experience of such things. On certain occasions, it's necessary to provide that chance, so that you can take a step back and make a new start in your life.'

As he stood up and held out his hand, he ended with a piece of advice:

'Get a job. Find a good woman and have lots of children. That's better than what you've been doing so far, living from day to day, aimlessly, at the mercy of thieves, murderers and thugs. What were you in your country?'

'Farmers.'

'So go back to your roots. Here's my card. If you need my help, there's my phone number. Good luck.'

Encinas left while both friends stood staring at his back and then looked down at the card he had left them.

'It's the first time a policeman has ever given me his card, Vasili.'

'Grigori.'

'Yes?'

'From now on, it would be best that we don't do anything to fuck things up again. Understood?'

***

Aaron Bukowski was satisfied. He had recovered the stolen drawing and had not had to pay another ransom. He was deeply saddened to learn that Superintendent Frutos had been the source of his misfortunes and that, moreover, he had met such a tragic end. Moreover, the betrayal of his housekeeper, Guadalupe, made him feel as if he had been stabbed twice over.

He was a man who advocated peace, harmony, friendship and respect, and yet, from time to time, he encountered people who behaved badly towards him. Fortunately, on this occasion he had been lucky enough to be able to count on the invaluable help of Daniel Olavarría, who had been generous enough not to present him with a bill for his services, something unusual for a man like Daniel.

Between Daniel and Bukowski's own international contacts, they had managed to recover the masterpiece that meant so much to him, and to do so without having to hand over more money. Moreover, they had succeeded in imprisoning the Qatari tycoon, a serial art trafficker, and all this in an unusually short time.

Being an irrepressible optimist, he decided to organise another of his dinners. This time he would, of course, invite Daniel, who would be the guest of honour. He would not mention that to him, though, because he would certainly refuse to come. And to join him, and to make him feel at home, he would invite the crème de la crème of Marbella, many of them personal friends of Daniel's and also of Aaron's. So, it would be like a party among friends, more relaxed and less formal than at other times.

Well-known entrepreneurs in the hotel business, owners of luxurious and exclusive clubs and restaurants, the odd banker, the occasional member of a royal family would all be there. In short: anyone who was anyone in Marbella.

He would have to make a list of the guests, contact them, check their availability, agree on a date, send them the formal invitation, design the menu, choose the wine... It was too much work. Before, all that was done by Guadeloupe, but her replacement had to be given time to settle into her new home and new routines. No. Aaron Bukowski came up with a better idea. He was going to do something he had never done before.

'Tomas, please,' he said to his butler. 'Get the phone number of the company *Destellos Marbella*. Then call and ask someone to organise a dinner party.'

On the day set for the dinner, Bukowski's villa was decked out in its best finery to match the illustrious guests who, at Aaron's specific request, abandoned formal attire in favour of more casual dress. Among the gentlemen, blazers and shirts without ties abounded. The ladies, too, left the bling and glitz at home, but designer outfits featured prominently that night.

Daniel was almost the last to arrive. Aaron had arranged for everyone else to be there an hour earlier. When he pulled up, Daniel found a splendidly decorated villa with, outside it, a line of chauffeurs and their limousines that seemed to go on forever. He thought he must have got the time wrong, given that so many people were already enjoying the party.

He rang the bell somewhat embarrassed at being the last to arrive, something he couldn't stand. In fact, he always hated being late for an appointment, but this one was special. The first thing he would do would be to make excuses to Bukowski.

He rang the bell, and the murmur of conversation that could be heard from outside suddenly subsided until it was almost inaudible. He was surprised that it took Tomas longer than usual to let him in, but he realised that he must be busier than ever that night. At last, the door opened and when Daniel stepped into the huge foyer, he found that all the guests were waiting for him and he was received with rapturous applause.

Daniel was baffled and the expression on his face said it all. He knew it was a dinner with friends, as Bukowski had told him, but he had not been told that there would be so many friends and that he would be greeted like a hero.

The host rushed over to rescue the distraught and confused Daniel from the discomfort he was in.

> 'My dear friend, welcome. We're delighted to have you here and indebted to you for your help. Please come in. I think you know everyone already, don't you?'
>
> 'Yes, I think so,' he said as he made his way towards the room where the gathering was being held and greeted everyone he passed.
>
> 'Please, from now on, everyone make yourself at home. The bar is over there and the bar staff are very attentive and helpful. There's still about half an hour before we sit down to eat, so take advantage of it and have something to drink.'
>
> 'After that welcome, I think I need a drink.'

He felt somewhat embarrassed. It wasn't that he was particularly shy but he was used to going about his work with complete discretion, and this was the antithesis. He was grateful to them, and especially to Bukowski, but in a way, this was all a bit too much.

He went up to the bar, staffed by charming, professional and beautiful waitresses, and ordered a whisky. As it was being prepared, he became aware of someone behind him tapping him on the shoulder.

'I hope you're off duty, Detective Olavarría.'

The person addressing him thus was Carmen, the Interpol commander. Daniel turned around and was taken aback.

Carmen was wearing a tight-fitting, deep red dress. Her green eyes stood out against her dark black hair and her lips matched her dress and shoes. She was a spectacularly beautiful woman.

'Wow, Commander, what a pleasant surprise!'

'Gosh! We've gone from Carmen to Commander.'

'I'm sorry, you're right. You just caught me off guard. I didn't expect to find you here. Besides, you're...'

'Yes?'

'Um, different.'

'Different?'

'Yes. Your hairstyle, your dress, your shoes... everything is different.'

'Does it meet with your approval?'

'Outstanding. You look really beautiful. And that threw me too,' he said as he stared at her.

'Thank you. It's just that when we first met each other we were in a different context. A professional, asexual, Arab one.'

'I confess that I prefer contexts like this one now. I love your dress.'

'Thank you, Daniel. It's one of those things we women decide to buy as we walk past a shop without thinking about whether we'll ever wear it.'

'I'm glad you did. And it's great to see you again. I've thought about you often and how much fun we had in Qatar that night we went out for dinner.'

'I had a great time too. And I've thought about you as well. So when Aaron called me and asked me if I was available, I said yes of course.'

'How do you know Bukowski?'

'Aaron and my father are good friends.'

'From now on, we won't talk about work, OK?'

Tomas got their attention by ringing a small gong:

'Ladies and gentlemen, dinner is served. Please take your seats.'

'Shall we sit together?' Daniel said.

'I'd love to.'

THE END

ABOUT THE AUTHOR

The author has spent his entire professional life working in Information Technology. However, he has had a passion for writing for many years, although he took the first steps into this new career almost by pure chance.

He has published several books. His works tell stories in which the characters are real flesh and blood people, easily recognisable, because they are our neighbours, friends, work colleagues or relatives, many of whom will have experienced similar circumstances to those described in his novels.